Her Greek Billionaire

Lucy Monroe

Lucy Monroe LLC

DEDICATION

For my daughter-in-law. Thank you, Megan, for being so dear and becoming a daughter of my heart. Your strong spirit, determination and tender heart remind me of Rowan. I hope you enjoy her book.

Chapter One

R owan Johnson pulled her five-year-old, ecofriendly electric compact to a stop in front of a mansion in one of the wealthiest neighborhoods in Athens.

The soaring stone wall that encompassed the huge property in its entirety was broken only by an imposing steel gate. Painted a sandy brown to match the stone in the wall, it was wide enough to let a delivery vehicle through. Right now, it was shut tight.

Taking a deep breath for courage, she got out of her little car. She wasn't going to back out now. This was what she wanted, and if she rightly read the way Lysander Baros, Greek billionaire and most eligible Athens bachelor, not to mention the sexiest one, looked at her, he did too.

Even if he didn't want it as much as she did, the chance to knock his half-brother down a peg might be worth it all on its own.

Rowen walked to the callbox beside the gate, stepping carefully in her three-inch heels. She wasn't dressed to go walking, or even to go out. She would never go to a club in a skirt as tight as the one on the dress she wore. Nor with a neckline as plunging.

She was dressed to seduce and hoped she'd gotten it right.

At thirty, she wasn't a virgin, but neither was she particularly experienced in the art of seduction. Married at the age of twenty and filing for divorce nine years later, there hadn't been a lot of time for her to learn. But she was ready to change that.

She was ready to show her ex, who thought the divorce had been her way of demanding fidelity, not ending their marriage, that she was moving on. And what better way than with the illegitimate half-brother who Cyrus regarded with equal parts jealousy and antipathy?

The fact that Rowan wanted Lysander in a way she'd never craved physical connection with Cyrus only made this little plan both possible and potentially pleasurable.

"Do you have an appointment?"

The voice startled Rowan out of her musings, and nearly toppled her off of her three-inch heels.

She spun around to see that while yes, there was a call box on one side of the gate like on the estate she'd once shared with her husband, there was also a security gate on the other. It was manned by a guard who looked like he knew what he was doing. She supposed that was the difference between security for a billionaire like Lysander Baros and a millionaire like his half-brother and her ex, Cyrus Andino.

"Um, no, but I think Lysander will see me." As she said the words, Rowan realized how foolish they sounded. This guard didn't know her, or that she knew Lysander.

It hadn't been very smart to come over here without calling Lysander first either. What if he was entertaining?

She knew he preferred quiet after returning from extended business trips, but that didn't mean he wouldn't have a discreet companion to welcome him home from his trip to Asia. He'd been gone seven weeks and visited five countries, with stops in multiple cities in each. A grueling schedule, even for a man like her Greek billionaire.

No, not *hers*. He would never be that, but he might be her lover if she handled this right.

The guard was looking at her impassively, and kudos to him for that because he had to have lots of experience turning away women who wanted a little of Lysander's time and were sure that he'd want to see them. Even if he weren't a billionaire, he would be in high demand with his square jawed good looks, wavy dark hair and utterly mesmerizing blue eyes. Not to mention a muscular body most athletes would envy.

Rowan grabbed her bag and dug out her phone. Much easier in the small, elegant bag she'd paired with her slinky designer dress than her usual hold all.

"Let me just call him and let him know I'm here," she said, looking up to give the guard a winning smile, only to find a gun trained on her.

Rowan screamed and dropped her phone.

Not a very practical reaction, she admitted, but she'd never seen a gun in person, much less had one pointed at her. Of course, she knew her security had been armed when she was married to Cyrus, but the guns had always been covered by suitcoats. Or maybe they'd worn ankle holsters?

She didn't know, and neither mattered now as she stared down the barrel of the gun still pointed at her.

Her initial shock wearing off, indignation set in, and she frowned severely at the security guard. "Why are you threatening me with a gun? How could that possibly be necessary?"

"I thought you might be going for a weapon," he said.

She didn't even try to hold back the snort of derision. "Clearly not." She pointed to the phone on the ground a few feet away. "I was trying to get my phone out so I could call Lysander and tell him I'm here."

"What is your name?" the guard asked.

"Rowan Johnson." She'd taken back her maiden name at the divorce.

The guard's expression didn't change. "Your name is not on the list."

"You haven't bothered to look at any list," she said, unimpressed.

"I have it memorized, and your name is not on it."

"Oh, do you have an eidetic memory? Only isn't being a gate guard an odd choice of careers for someone with that kind of skill?" she asked herself more than him.

Rowan always wanted to understand the why of people. It was hard-wired into her. At least that's how it felt to her.

"I'm a security specialist, and no I don't have a photographic memory. Mr. Baros's list of approved guests is short."

"Oh. That's not surprising, I guess. I can't help noticing your gun is still pointed at me." And it was making her nervous. Well, strictly speaking, she'd gotten a full dose of scared and worried the second the gun came out.

There was no making about it.

"I haven't yet ascertained if you are a threat."

"Look, how about you call Lysander and tell him Rowan Johnson nee Andino is at the gate?"

"I cannot do that."

"Why not? Did you drop your cell phone too?" she asked sarcastically, but inside she was shaking a little. Her phone was only a few feet away, but she wasn't about to move toward it while he had his gun out.

What kind of security was trained to threaten violence without the least provocation? Rowan wasn't feeling sexy anymore. She was angry and scared, and that only made her angrier.

"Policy is not to bother Mr. Baros with anyone showing up who does not have an appointment."

"Okay, fine. Put your gun away and I will get my cell phone and call him."

"Show me the inside of your purse first," the man instructed.

It was a rude request, and surely unnecessary, but Rowan wanted that gun put away more than she wanted to argue about the invasion of her privacy.

So, she opened her small clutch and turned it so he could see the inside. "There. No weapons of any kind. I don't even carry a nail file with me. Satisfied?"

He nodded and holstered his gun.

Rowan surged forward to grab her phone, forgetting she was wearing heels rather than her usual more sensible foot attire and promptly twisted her ankle, falling forward to land heavily on her knees. She cried out and then gasped as sharp pricks of pain from her skinned knees and a resounding throb in her ankle assailed her.

Shoot. This was the worst plan ever. What had she been thinking?

Seduce Mr. Sexy himself and make sure Cyrus heard about it so he would stop hounding her about reconciling? She wanted to get her dad and brothers off her back as well. They were business partners with her ex and apparently the divorce had made things uncomfortable for them.

Like that was all that mattered. But considering the fact they'd all known Cyrus slept around during her marriage and had never told her, there could be no question where their loyalty lay.

Anyway, this plan was definitely a bust. Climbing to her feet without flashing her panties was the kind of struggle she'd never thought to face and told her why she never dressed in this kind of clothing. She was far too clutzy for femme fatale gear.

Taking a step, she nearly fell again from the pain. No way could she walk another step in these heels, much less back to her car. Leaning against the wall, she removed first one sandal and then the other. Then she limped to her phone, her ire getting worse with every painful step.

When she reached the phone, she was faced with another dilemma. How did she bend down to get it without her skirt riding up indecently? If she tried to squat, she'd be equally exposed but in a different area of her anatomy.

Finally, she managed a combination squat-bend and got the phone.

She unlocked it and called Lysander.

"Hello, Rowan, what an unexpected pleasure," he said in his smooth, deep voice answering after the second ring.

"So, you have my number in your phone, but my name isn't on your list. I can't believe I thought having sex with you was a good idea. You have your guards trained to pull guns on people just for trying to use their phones? What kind of man is that paranoid?"

"What are you saying? You aren't making sense."

"You're right. My idea was completely nonsensical but I don't think I needed to pay for that with skinned knees, a twisted ankle and having a gun drawn on me."

"Slow down, Rowan, who drew a gun on you?"

"Your gate guard, excuse me, *security specialist*," she emphasized. "He scared the bejeebees out of me. I don't like wearing heels."

"I know. You mentioned it once when we were dancing."

He'd asked her to dance at one of the dos for a charity both her ex and Lysander had supported. That the two men agreed on even that was almost a miracle. She'd learned that after the dance though. When Cyrus had berated her for dancing with the other man.

"But he's your brother."

"My half-brother. Why my father chose to acknowledge him, I'll never understand, but we aren't legal family."

Which meant what? She'd always wondered. They weren't legal brothers, but they shared half their DNA and they'd been raised by the same father, though saying Baptiste Andino had had a hand in raising his mistress's child was a bit of a stretch. But he had acknowledged Lysander as his son publicly and paid for his support and schooling, something that Cyrus resented. The connection had never been a secret. Her ex had resented that too.

Rowan had quickly learned that Cyrus took it as a personal affront if Rowan so much as smiled at Lysander, much less talked to him. Cyrus had frozen her out for a week after that innocent dance.

"We have only danced once," she pointed out now. "And trust me the exercise isn't likely to be repeated. I'm totally off men who have their security trained to treat visitors to their estate like the international most wanted."

"Gregor will bring you to the house." Then the call dropped. How rude. He hadn't even said goodbye.

Suddenly the gate started to slide open, and the security specialist headed toward her with rapid steps. His gun was still holstered, but the look on his face showed intent. Rowan just knew that intent had something to do with her.

Just how ridiculous her plan was washed over Rowan and filled her with embarrassment. Why had she thought Mr. Eligible Bachelor himself would want to sleep with her when he could have pretty much any woman, or man if he swung that way, in Athens? Like heck she was sticking around so he could laugh in her face at the very idea.

She took a step toward her car and nearly fell again. Crud, that had hurt.

Her knees were still stinging and any movement made the pain more acute, but it was her ankle that was making walking difficult. She limped as fast as she could, but hadn't yet reached her car when a hand came around her wrist like a manacle.

She gasped and yanked against the hold instinctively. Her wrist remained firmly in the security specialist's grip.

"Mr. Baros would like you to come to the house so he can speak to you." The guard's tone was polite, but that didn't make her any less his prisoner.

"Mr. Baros can call me at his convenience. I want to leave," Rowan said tartly. "Let go of my hand."

Even if she still thought her idea was a good one, and she didn't, she had no desire to meet up with Lysander with skinned knees, a sore ankle and a sweaty brow from stress.

Chapter Two

"Please be reasonable, Miz Johnson. You came here to see Mr. Baros. If you come with me, you can do that."

"I would rather go home."

"Klaus is bringing your car up to the house already."

Sure enough, her little electric car was being driven through the gate by a man as large as the one in possession of her wrist, but with blond hair. He grinned at her and tipped an imaginary hat in her direction through the window of her car.

"Hey, you can't steal my car," she shouted at him. To no effect.

"He's not stealing it. He is merely parking it for you. It is a courtesy," Gregor said, his own expression as impassive as it had been since the beginning of their discussion.

However, there was something around his eyes. Something that told her he was amused by this situation. Rowan was not.

"How am I supposed to get up to the house? I don't know if it escaped your notice, but I twisted my ankle."

"I saw." No apology for his part in her debacle, just an admission he'd seen it happen.

She glared at him. "So?"

"I have a vehicle here." He helped her over to a vehicle that might have been a golf cart in another life. In this one, it was painted a discreet grey with the logo of a security firm emblazoned on the side.

The ride up to the house was a short one. When they arrived at the front door, there was no sign of her compact.

"Where is my car?" she asked.

"Klaus has parked it in an empty garage bay." The answer did not come from Gregor.

Butterflies waged war in Rowan's tummy like peaceful, innocent butter-flies were not supposed to do and Rowan turned her head to see the object of her visit. And quite a few of her recent fantasies.

Lysander Baros. He stood there in a pair of slacks and white dress shirt, sleeves rolled up to reveal the tanned skin and defined muscles of his forearms. The top two buttons of his shirt were undone, and she could see a hint of his dark chest hair.

Despite the situation she'd found herself in, her body had a predictable response to this man. The same response she'd had to every image she saw of him, or the rare times she saw him at an event in person since her divorce. She wanted him. She'd never wanted Cyrus this way and the fact was that she didn't want any other man like this either.

It was like her body had tuned to Lysander's station and everything else was static.

Nevertheless, the utmost emotion in Rowan at the moment was anger.

Uncertain if she could stand at the minute, she didn't try to get out of her seat in the security vehicle. Instead, she turned her body so he could receive the full weight of her displeasure. "Well, he can just unpark it and bring it back round. I want to go home."

"But you came to see me, yes? And here I am."

"What? Do you want a gold star for participation, or something? First, you have your goon pull a gun on me. Then you hang up on me without saying goodbye. That is rude and I know your mom taught you better. She's a nice lady."

Lysander's eyes widened at Rowan's tone, but he didn't say anything.

So, she continued. "Then you send another goon to steal my car." She ticked each offense with one finger. She had three fingers up so far. "But that wasn't enough? No, you had to have your—"

"Goon," Gregor supplied helpfully, cutting into her words.

She let him have some of her ire filled gaze before turning her attention back to the man who had infuriated her to the point of raising her voice. "Right, your goon—"

"His name is Gregor," Klaus said, coming up, his expression showing all the humor he found in the current situation.

Rowan crossed her arms over her chest and frowned at him this time. "You'll notice I'm not laughing. Your boss had me kidnapped and that is not only illegal, it's—"

"Let me guess, rude?" Gregor asked, his own tone now showing his amusement as well.

"So is interrupting people."

"You'll have to forgive me, I grew up in an orphanage and the streets of Athens. No mother to teach me polite behavior."

"Goodness help you then, because clearly you aren't going to learn it from your boss."

Both the security specialists laughed out loud at that.

Which made Rowan feel just a tiny bit vindicated. They didn't mind seeing the arrogant self-made billionaire taken down a peg. Funny, but before today she'd had no desire to see that herself. Apparently wealthy men forgot what they learned in manners in their pursuit of money.

Maybe she should write an op-ed about that. She wondered if any of the fringe press would publish it.

"You were saying," Lysander prompted when Rowan had been lost in silent thought for several seconds.

"Oh, uh, right. I want to go home."

"You said you had skinned knees and a twisted ankle?" he asked, sounding solicitous, if she could believe that.

She didn't. "Yes, because you have your goons—"

"I prefer security specialist," Klaus said.

Rowan felt like a tea kettle about to go off. She never screamed shrilly, but these men. They thought they were so cute. "Seriously? Act like a security specialist and that's what I'll call you. Act like a goon and that's your title."

"I didn't do anything goonish," Klaus said, all innocence.

"You stole my car."

"I parked it for you. I often park guest's cars for Mr. Baros."

"So, you're a valet, not a security specialist?" she asked with raised brows.

"Apparently, he's both," Lysander said, finally speaking. "I apologize that my security specialists' methods were distressing for you, but I would appreciate you allowing me to have your wounds seen to."

"They're not wounds." That sounded so serious.

But Lysander wasn't listening. He was in fact, sliding one strong arm under her hips and the other behind her back. Rowan let out a squeak she would deny later having made as she was lifted right against the rock-solid chest that had played a pivotal role in several fantasies of late.

"Now you're kidnapping me?" she asked with more breathlessness than she would ever admit to, and very little of the ire she'd intended.

"You have not been kidnapped. You came to see me. You see me. Klaus did not steal your car. It is waiting for you safely in the estate garage." He said nothing about Gregor drawing his gun on her, but Lysander had already said he was sorry she'd found it distressing.

Like that was the end of it, like a simple apology could make up for her terror at having a weapon pointed at her for no reason at all.

"If you aren't kidnapping me, then put me down and have my car brought back around."

"We have yet to see your wounds doctored," he replied.

"They're hardly wounds. Just..." She wasn't sure what to classify her skinned knees as. Saying owie felt rather juvenile, especially with how her body was responding to his in such a very adult manner. "Do you ever listen?" she demanded, even as she tried to steady her breathing.

"I listen to you. I distinctly heard you say you want to have sex with me." His deep tone held a wealth of satisfaction.

"Of course, you heard that and ignored everything else I said." Typical man.

"I do not ignore you, but surely you did not come all this way simply to turn around without having the discussion you hoped to with me."

"That was not my original plan, no, but it became my plan after Gregor pulled his gun on me."

"So, you do remember his name."

"Seriously, Lysander. Do you really have such a problem with women showing up at your gate that pulling guns on unexpected visitors is your people's go to?"

Lysander shook his head. "We have had some threats."

"What do you mean we?" She tried to read his handsome features. "Do you mean you? Someone is threatening you and in a serious enough way that you've got your security on high alert?"

The thought of someone doing him harm sent a wave of dread over her.

"I cut business ties with and funding for a group with ties to shady, but powerful businessmen who want to see clean energy regulations loosened or done away with altogether."

Lysander's support of the EU's stance on clean energy was well known. It was one of the things she liked about him.

"And they think threatening you will get you to do business with them again?" she asked incredulously. She and Lysander were not close, but he was a force to be reckoned with in the business world, not someone to be intimidated.

"Intimidation might work for someone without my security resources," he said with a shrug as they entered an inviting living area, and no mention of his powerful influence in the global world of business.

Rowan let her gaze scan the room. This was not an entertaining space for business contacts. Family photos made up a collage on one wall Rowan was sure was courtesy of Iona Baros, Lysander's mom. She'd never taken him to be the sentimental type, but the photos were there, regardless of who had them framed and hung.

A large screen television was on and paused on a stock report. There was an oversized chocolate brown sectional sofa with lots of cushions and a square coffee table that held a coffee cup and a tablet.

This had been where Lysander was when she'd called him. He'd probably been reading the news on his tablet while listening to the stock report on the TV. He laid her on the chaise lounge part of the sectional and sat down beside her, their hips touching, and his body oriented to face hers.

"This is a cozy room," Rowan observed.

"My private sanctum."

Before he could add anything else, like why he'd brought Rowan in here rather than a more public room in the mansion, a woman dressed in the no nonsense uniform of a housekeeper with her salt and pepper hair pulled back into a severe bun briskly walked in. She carried a laden tray. She spoke in rapid Greek to Lysander, telling him she had the supplies to tend to his guest.

Clearly expecting her boss to move out of the way, the housekeeper stepped toward Rowan. However, Lysander put his hand out with an imperious gesture. "Give it to me."

"You are going to put bandages on my skinned knees?" Rowan asked with shock. *He* was?

"Not until I have cleaned them," he said, like that should be self-evident. "But first let us get some ice on your ankle. Which one is paining you?"

Rowan pointed to her left ankle, which did not look swollen, so she had hopes it wasn't a full-on sprain.

He laid a cloth neatly over her ankle and then carefully placed an icepack on top of the cloth before instructing a smart speaker to set a twenty-minute timer. "Do you want something for the pain?"

"If you have a couple of ibuprofen, I'll happily take them." At some point she would have to walk out of here on her own steam. She'd like to be able to do that without making an absolute cake of herself.

Lysander sent the housekeeper for the ibuprofen and then took a damp cloth from a pile of neatly rolled ones just like it and dabbed oh so gently at her left knee. It still stung and Rowan winced.

He blew on it. "Better?"

Unable to form even the single word *yes*, Rowan gulped and nodded.

CHAPTER THREE

The housekeeper returned with a tumbler of water and two tablets. Thanking the other woman in Greek, Rowan took the pain relievers with a sip of water.

"Drink at least a cup. It is better for you and will make the pain reliever work faster," Lysander instructed.

Rowan did as directed because she knew he was right, not because she was usually amenable to being bossed around. Even for her own good.

Lysander repeated the gentle dabbing to her knee with the wet cloth, then soft blowing to take the sting away until he was apparently satisfied with the results of his ministrations. He then put some ointment on the abrasion before picking out the perfect sized bandage and applying it. After he had shown her right knee equally careful attention, he moved the tray from the sofa to the coffee table.

However, he made no move to put any physical distance between them.

"How is your ankle feeling?" he asked.

She shrugged. "The ice seems to be helping."

"We'll check it after the timer goes off and determine if you need a doctor to look at it."

"Oh, I'm sure that's not necessary," she assured him. "It didn't look swollen."

He made a noncommittal noise.

"I do not like going to the doctor's," she informed him. Her antipathy was rooted in a childhood spent in too many doctor's offices monitoring a heart condition that had required surgery when she was six.

Since then, her heart was the strongest muscle in her body, she was sure of it. It would have to be to survive the betrayal of both her husband and her family.

"Understood," Lysander said.

"What does that mean? You understand I don't want to go to the doctor's office, but I'm going anyway if you think my ankle needs attention?" she asked with heavy sarcasm.

He gave her a slashing white smile. "It is like you know me, but not exactly. I understand if your ankle needs attention, my concierge doctor will be called to attend you here."

"You have a concierge doctor?" Of course, he did. He was a billionaire after all.

"It is a matter of time, efficiency, and security."

"Does it ever bother you?"

"What?"

"That you cannot live like a normal person. If you run out of milk, going to the grocery store means taking a whole entourage of security and staff?"

"First, I don't care for dairy milk. Second, I would never think to go to the grocery store. Helen would be appalled at my choices, I am sure."

She'd heard him call the housekeeper, Helen. "Your housekeeper, not your cook?"

"Helen rules the house," he said with a shrug. "Even Etienne would not think to oppose her."

"Etienne is your chef?"

"He is. He makes an even better moussaka than Mama, but if you tell her I said so, I will deny it."

Rowan laughed as she knew she was meant to.

"Your divorce has become final?" he asked, apropos of nothing.

Though considering she'd told him she wanted sex with him, maybe not nothing.

"Yes, last week." Since she'd been married in the USA, she'd filed in a US court, but it had still taken over a year to finalize.

Her ex had not been cooperative. Lucky for her, his infidelity had been easy to document and the divorce laws in her home state favored her petition. She also hadn't asked for maintenance, or a financial settlement.

The prenuptial agreement she'd signed had dictated certain financial arrangements she'd been happy to forego for her freedom from the marriage. The judge presiding had not agreed and had ordered a fulfillment of the contract to the letter.

Cyrus and her own family had been livid, but now she had a nest egg. She was still deciding how much of it she intended to keep, and how much she would donate to causes close to her heart.

With her degree in human resources, Rowan was perfectly capable of supporting herself, if not in the lifestyle she'd known growing up or during her marriage, in one she found comfortable.

Lysander smiled at her answer. "Good."

"That's not the usual response I get." Mostly people told her they were sorry. She was sorry too, not to be divorced, but that she'd ever been duped by Cyrus to begin with.

Lysander shrugged. "You were not happy in your marriage even before you found out that Cyrus had broken his marriage vows."

"That's a very old-fashioned way of putting it," she said.

"I am an old-fashioned man in some ways. I believe promises are meant to be kept. It is why I never intend to marry."

She didn't believe for a minute he was engaging in idle chit-chat. He was warning her. Sex might be in the offing, but commitment wasn't.

"Don't worry, Lysander, I'm not looking for another husband." Rowan didn't believe all men were lying cheaters like her ex, but Lysander had been right. She hadn't been happy in her marriage long before she'd learned of Cyrus's ongoing and frequent extra-marital bedroom activities.

"I don't think I'm cut out for marriage," she told Lysander with more honesty than was probably smart to engage in. "I didn't enjoy having my *I* constantly subsumed by the *we*."

"I do not believe all marriages require that, but I am by no means an expert, having never been married and being the product of a relationship that was never going to include that particular element."

"Did that bother you?" she asked, wondering even as she did so if he would deign to answer.

It was a cheekily personal question.

"There were times in my life it bothered me a great deal," he said surprising her with his honesty. "Now is not one of them."

"What changed?"

"I made a place for myself in the world where it does not matter."

"I would have to agree." Lysander wielded influence his brother and even his father could not hope to match.

It infuriated Cyrus, making him jealous and mean about the sibling he refused to acknowledge in any meaningful way.

"It clearly does not matter to you," he said, a wealth of meaning in his words.

Heat climbed into Rowan's cheeks. Why had she said that about wanting to have sex with him?

"You do realize having a gun pointed at me was a real turn off, don't you?" she asked repressively.

His gaze skimmed down her body, noting she was sure the way her beaded nipples pressed against the thin fabric of her barely there bra and slinky dress. "Funnily enough, no, it had not occurred to me."

Before she could make a blistering retort, or at least say something about looks being deceiving, the alarm on the smart speaker went off.

"Time to check your ankle," he said, shifting so he could lift the cloth and icepack to reveal her foot and ankle closest to him.

He trailed his fingertip from the tip of her big toe over her foot and up her ankle. "How does that feel?"

"F..." She coughed. "Fine."

"Try rotating your foot."

She did and felt only the tiniest twinge. Oh, thank goodness, it really was going to be fine and there would be no need for wrapping or crutches.

"Let us see how you do putting weight on it." He suited action to words, standing up and holding his hands out to her.

She grasped them and stood, relief flooding her when the twinge didn't grow into a throb. "I should have no trouble walking on it now. Thank you. Did you want to have my car brought round?"

He shook his head.

She cocked her head to one side, eyeing him warily. "I'm still a kidnap victim then?"

"We still have your original reason for coming to visit to discuss."

"I think I'd rather discuss it sometime when I haven't been accosted by your goons." If ever. The reality of what she'd planned to propose to him was hitting her hard.

Had Rowan really thought suggesting they have sex to stick it to her ex was a good idea?

"I would prefer to discuss it now," he said with certainty. "You came dressed so enticingly and for my benefit, how can I do anything but give you my full attention?"

"I'm sure I'm not the first woman who showed up at your gate dressed to seduce."

"You're the first one I have any interest in though."

"Oh."

"This chemistry between us, it goes both ways." He touched her face with his fingertips.

That small connection sent electric shocks through Rowan's body. If she'd responded this way to her ex, maybe their marriage wouldn't have been such a sham. Instantly shaking off those thoughts, Rowan reminded herself that her former husband's choices had not been her fault. He'd never been faithful, not from the very beginning, as his longtime mistress had been happy to point out.

The other woman hadn't been his only extramarital relationship, so she probably had her own axe to grind. Delphine had insisted that powerful men like Cyrus could not be expected to be faithful.

Maybe Rowan was naïve, but she *had* expected her Greek husband to honor his promise of fidelity.

Delphine had only been too happy to provide evidence against Cyrus in the divorce. Perhaps because he'd lied to her once too often?

Rowan didn't know and neither did she care. Her life with Cyrus was over and this, right here, this was how she intended to show that to the world.

"I don't think you'll like my stipulations," she said now to Lysander.

His expression instantly wary, he asked, "What stipulations?"

"In the morning, or whatever time I leave in the night, I want to be caught by the paparazzi."

"You want to have sex with me to have revenge on your ex?" Lysander asked.

She couldn't tell from his tone how he felt about that. His expression wasn't a happy one, but then Lysander wasn't known for his affable personality. Gorgeous? Check. Uber wealthy. Double check. Personable? Sometimes. But he was more aloof than charming. In fact, she would have called him downright grumpy, though no one else seemed willing to.

"I want to have sex with you because I want you. I want the paparazzi to catch me so my ex-husband will realize the divorce wasn't some kind of feminine plea for fidelity."

"He doesn't accept that your marriage is over?" Lysander asked.

"Not even a little. He sent me roses just yesterday. I gave them to my neighbor."

"You do not like roses?"

"I love them, but I don't like the sender. I want him out of my life completely, only my family and he still have dreams of dynasty building. They're all sure that once I start having babies everything will fall into place."

"You were married ten years."

"Nine. Our marriage ended when I learned of his infidelity."

"But the divorce only finalized last week."

"Yes. Now it isn't just a matter of how I see my life, but that I am legally no longer bound to him in any way."

"My point was that if they are looking for dynasty building, a marriage that did not produce children in nearly a decade is not one likely to in the future either."

"I was on birth control for the first few years."

"And after?"

She sighed. "We didn't have sex that often and it just never happened." Now she was really glad it hadn't. Rowan couldn't imagine being tied to Cyrus Andino indefinitely through a child.

But for a while, her lack of motherhood had been a real source of grief for her.

"So, not dynasty building," Lysander said, almost musingly.

Chapter Four

"What do you mean?" Rowan asked Lysander.

"Cyrus wants you back. It could be as simple as not being willing to let go of what he believes is his, but the fact you didn't have children and he is narcissistic enough to insist on leaving his imprint on the next generation, leads to an important question."

"What would that be?"

"Why won't he let you go? Of course, he may well know the fertility problem lies with him already. He has no children with any of his lovers either. Not even Delphine, and they've been together since before your wedding."

"You knew all this?" she asked, feeling betrayed. Only Lysander hadn't betrayed her.

They hadn't been considered family. Their combustible chemistry aside, they weren't even friends. He hadn't owed her the truth. Not like her own family, all of whom had been aware of Delphine, if not Cyrus's other pillow friends.

"How?" she asked.

"I keep tabs on my family, especially the ones who would prefer I did not exist."

Rowan couldn't deny that interpretation of Cyrus's feelings.

"You're more than a little paranoid, aren't you?" She hadn't forgotten his goon drawing his gun on her, even if Lysander preferred to pretend it hadn't happened.

"I am cautious, that is all. And I have good reason to be. Cyrus is not a good man."

"I wish someone had said as much to me before I married him," Rowan muttered.

"Had I known you, I would have."

She believed him. "But Cyrus and I met in the States and that's where we got married." After a whirlwind courtship, that looking back on, had all sorts of red flags.

But her family had been all in on the idea of her marrying an Andino and Rowan had been completely taken in by Cyrus's charm and good looks. He'd known just what to say and how to act. Of course, at the time she'd had no idea he'd been getting coaching from her own father.

"Tell me about your prenuptial agreement."

"Are you saying you haven't managed to get yourself a copy?"

"I admit I never even tried. It was of little interest to me. You, the most intriguing woman I'd met, were married to my detestable half-brother."

Rowan hadn't been the only one avoiding Lysander since that dance. He'd done a good job of avoiding her as well. The feelings she had around him confused her and only later had she realized they were attracted to each other. By then, she'd been grateful for his discretion. Unlike her ex, Rowan had considered her wedding vows inviolate.

"Why do you want to hear about it now?"

"Because you assume that learning you have had sex with me will end Cyrus's interest in you. Forgive me, but my brother clearly didn't appreciate what he had in you when you were married, why so adamant now to get you back?"

"And you think something in the prenuptial agreement explains it?"

"Yes."

"Okay. You can read it. I'll send over a copy after I get home."

"Why not move back to the States?" he asked. "You went back to get the divorce?"

"I'm thirty years old," she told him. "I built a life for myself here in Athens. I have a job, even if it's one neither my family, nor Cyrus ever considered much of."

"You work as a career counselor for women going back into the workforce after a prolonged absence."

"Yes, and I find it very rewarding. I believe in what my organization does. I like my coworkers. My boss doesn't hover. My apartment isn't big, but it has a great view, and I can walk to work and all the shops from there. I have friends that are closer than my brother and sister are to me. This is where my life is, and Cyrus isn't chasing me out of Athens."

Besides, moving back to the US wasn't going to make it harder for Cyrus to pursue her. He had a private jet and spent at least one week a month in New York on business.

No, she had to get him (and her father) to understand without a doubt that she had moved on and wasn't ever going to be amenable to reconciliation. If she still loved Cyrus, that would make her decision harder, but once he'd stopped playing the part of perfect man for her, she'd discovered they had almost nothing in common and certainly nothing of substance.

"Cyrus wants me back because he doesn't like losing. Full stop."

"Tell me, was there a clause in the prenup that ensured you retained ownership of all gifts given to you over the course of your marriage?"

"There might have been. I only read the document once. I didn't ask for it to be enforced in the divorce."

"But it was?" Lysander asked.

"Yes. The judge decreed that all stipulations and clauses would be adhered to the letter."

"As I thought. It is likely that Cyrus put things in your name as a tax shelter, or even to hide their existence. Now you have ownership and I am guessing it impacts his business in a seriously negative way if he doesn't get control of those assets back. Did you get shares in his company as part of the divorce settlement."

That she *could* answer. "Yes. I got ten percent of his company and he got ten percent of my father's company, but now that the divorce is finalized, us getting remarried isn't going to change that."

"It could."

"If he convinced me to sign them over."

"Both your father and Cyrus have reason to want that outcome."

"Then you think if I sign the shares back over to Cyrus, he'll stop trying to pursue me?" She'd wanted to donate them to her organization as an ongoing source of income, but if it meant getting Cyrus out of her life entirely, she'd give them back in a hot minute.

Or would she? There was a lot of good that could be done with that money and Cyrus was never going to do it.

"It depends."

"Right. You think he may have put other assets in my name."

"It's almost a certainty. He is too short sighted to realize that he would not always have control of you, much less those assets that legally now belong to you."

"That does sound like Cyrus. What if I give it all back? Then he'll leave me alone."

"Is that what you really want?"

"I wanted to do some good with the money I got out of the divorce. I didn't ask for it, but it is mine and I thought I could make a difference."

"You still can."

"Once I give it all away, he won't have any reason to keep after me either," she said, realizing that was the truth. Oh, Cyrus, not to mention her father, would be furious.

She'd no doubts that they had some kind of deal to exchange the shares in each other's company if they succeeded in pressuring her into remarrying him. Not that she expected Cyrus would honor his side of the bargain. Her father was a fool if he did, but that was his lookout.

"So, this isn't necessary," she mused aloud.

"No, I don't think it is." Lysander gave her one of his rare slashing grins. "Not for the sake of ridding you of Cyrus, anyway."

And suddenly, she wasn't thinking about how to get rid of her ex, but what it would feel like to have Lysander's hands on her body, to have license to touch him as much as she liked. Those thoughts made her heart race.

Her mouth opened and a small puff of air expelled from her chest.

She wanted him.

And it didn't have a darn thing to do with revenge.

"I'm not married anymore." That felt like something important to say right then.

"No, you are not. I do not have a lover at present either."

"You don't sleep with more than one woman at the same time?" she asked, not sure she'd believe him if Lysander said no.

He shook his head. "I do not. I have had many lovers, but never more than one at a time."

"You don't do commitment."

"No, but I do temporary fidelity when the sex goes beyond a single night."

"What about Adele Fournier?" The French supermodel had been photographed on Lysander's arm several times over the past couple of years.

"Adele and I have a mutually beneficial arrangement. She likes to attend the functions I have to for business."

"Are you saying you never sleep with her?"

"I am saying that there is no expectation of commitment or fidelity on either side."

"The billionaire's version of friends with benefits." Of course, his *friend* was considered one of the most beautiful women in the world.

"While I find Adele's company less irritating than some, I would not say we are friends."

Why didn't that surprise her? Rowan wondered if the Greek tycoon considered anyone an actual friend.

Regardless, she wasn't looking for long term either. She was in fact, only proposing one night.

However, the knowledge that if they started something that lasted longer, he would not be sleeping with other women as well resonated. It settled inside her with a much stronger positive vibe than she would have expected it to.

It was like that mattered. A lot. And really? It shouldn't matter at all.

Her plan was to get rid of her ex once and for all, but also to prove to herself that she could move on. That the bad choice she'd made at twenty didn't have to define the rest of her life.

"I expect the same," he said almost warningly.

She thought about that. She didn't desire anyone but him and couldn't imagine jumping from his bed to someone else's. "I'm not sure why we're discussing this."

"We are getting the expectations out of the way before anything happens between us."

"You mean sex."

"I mean sex."

She sighed. "This feels very calculated."

"Did the prenup you signed before marriage feel calculated?" he asked.

"No, but that was different. People in our world sign prenuptial agreements all the time."

"And people discuss expectations before going to bed together." His hand slid around to cup the back of her neck, his thumb rubbing up and down softly against her skin. "Stay with me today. We'll watch a movie, have dinner in and relax together. Whatever happens, happens."

That sounded way better than a calculated move to the bedroom. "You watch movies?" she asked, infusing her voice with humor laced skepticism.

"Sometimes."

"Not often, I bet."

"No, not often, but even self-made billionaires have to have down time."

"I thought your version of down time was doing business in your shirt sleeves. I mean, correct me if I'm wrong, but you were in here reading the business news while listening to the stock market reports." She looked toward the television that was still paused on the screen showing a graph for stock prices on a global tech company.

"Caught, but I'm happy to pivot to something entirely nonwork related."

"What kind of movies do you like?" she asked, really curious.

"Documentaries are my favorite, but I indulge in action adventure too."

"I love documentaries. Have you watched the latest on hummingbirds?"

"I haven't had the pleasure."

"Neither have I, but my coworker said it's amazing."

He leaned down and grabbed the remote. "See if you can find it. I'll organize some refreshments."

"I'd love something bright and fizzy, but no alcohol." Being around him was enough of a challenge to her equilibrium without adding wine or hard liquor to the mix.

Chapter Five

"Something bright and fizzy coming right up." He grabbed his phone and sent a text.

She did a search for the documentary she wanted to watch and found it on the first try. She clicked into it and then paused it, so they could get comfortable before starting the show.

"I wish I'd worn more practical clothing," she lamented. "I don't think femme fatale is really in my repertoire."

"You look amazing, but maybe not very comfortable."

"I'm not." She tugged down the hem on her skirt which seemed to want to ride up. "Who knew dressing to seduce could be so irritating?"

She never would have twisted her ankle if she'd been wearing her normal shoes.

"Tell me your sizes and I'll get something delivered."

"What? No. That's a waste of energy and money when I have perfectly good clothing at home."

"But I want you to stay here, and I want you to be comfortable. You like that designer?" he asked, referring to her dress.

"Usually, yes." The dress she was wearing was from a different line than she usually shopped. And now that she was supporting herself, she needed to eschew designer labels all together.

If she did keep the money and assets she'd gotten from her divorce, she wasn't using them to continue supporting a lifestyle that had never made her happy. She liked hanging out with her friends in places that did not get written up in the social pages, or go viral on social media. She liked her little apartment and her neighbors that came from so many different walks of life.

"Give me a moment and I'll take care of it."

"Wouldn't it be easier to simply give my apartment key to one of your goons and send them to pick up some clothes for me?"

He shrugged. "There is nothing difficult about sending a personal shopper out for some outfits for you to choose from."

"You live in a very rarified world." Even more rarified than the one she'd known most of her life.

They settled on the couch after that, he insisting she put her ankle up on a cushion on the chaise. She didn't mind because it gave her some breathing room with the attraction threatening to overwhelm her. Not a lot, because he sat right beside her, but it wasn't instant sexy times.

They started watching the documentary on the hummingbirds. Despite having the most tantalizing man she'd ever known only inches away, Rowan quickly found herself engrossed. The housekeeper came in with drinks for them. Rowan's turned out to be a splash of cranberry and pineapple juice mixed with club soda and served over ice. It was refreshing and the cookies brought with it delicious.

Lysander put his arm around her shoulder and she let herself relax against him. As much as she was enjoying the documentary, this closer proximity soon began to wreak havoc with her senses. The heat of his body so close, the hard muscles of his chest pressing against her arm and shoulder, the scent that was so much more than the masculine aftershave he wore.

She shifted to get closer, inhaling that delicious smell that was all Lysander Baros and felt her skirt sliding up her legs. Darn it.

Vowing never to wear this dress again, she tugged her hem down, squirming as she did so.

"You really are uncomfortable in that dress," he said, sounding surprised.

"I thought I wouldn't be wearing it long," she admitted and then wished she hadn't.

He already knew she wanted him. He didn't need more proof.

"If things had gone according to your plan, you wouldn't have," he said with certainty. "I want to touch you badly."

"But I like that we're not just jumping into bed," she admitted.

"Not all sex happens in the bedroom." The tone of his voice made her look away from the beautiful little birds fighting over territory on the screen and up at him.

He was looking at her, specifically at how much of her curvy breasts were on display with her plunging neckline. She wasn't model thin, or anything close to it. Her tummy wasn't flat, and her butt filled out a pair of jeans very nicely. Her large breasts would easily fill his hands.

At six and a half feet tall, Lysander had big hands. And the thought of them on her body made Rowan's nipples tingle.

"I've never had sex outside of a bedroom," she admitted, just a little breathless at the idea.

Sure, she'd read about it. Books made lots of things seem possible that she'd never experienced in real life. Like a happy marriage. Like parents that put their children's happiness above their own desire for money, power and prestige. Like passion and fun and lots of other stuff besides.

Stuff that felt all to possible when she was with this man.

Lysander Baros.

His eyes had darkened, looking nearly black, his expression intent. "Never?"

Incapable of speech, Rowan shook her head.

Lysander pulled his phone out and sent a text. "We will not be disturbed." Then he got up and pulled thickly paneled pocket doors together, closing off the entrance to his sanctum from the hall. He crossed the room and shut another pocket door, closing off the entry the housekeeper had used earlier. "We are now entirely private."

"What about when my clothes arrive."

"I've instructed they be delivered to my bedroom."

"Oh, that's efficient." But hadn't the idea been for her to change into something less sexy for their television time?

He rejoined her on the sectional, shocking her when he settled them back into the position they'd been before. "Relax, watch the show. If your skirt rides up, no one is here to see it."

"You're here."

"Yes, I am." The meaning behind his words sent heat pulsing through her body.

Yes. He was. And that was what she wanted. To be here with him.

They went back to watching the show and Rowan felt herself relaxing again. When she shifted and her skirt inched up her thighs, she didn't worry about it. In fact, it excited her a little, just thinking he could see her body.

The idea of exposing her thighs to her husband had always stressed Rowan out. Cyrus always had something to say, and it was never complimentary. He'd made cutting comments about choosing a different designer for her clothes and not showing skin if it was dimpled with cellulite.

Why didn't she worry that Lysander would be turned off by her less than perfect body?

Maybe because despite him never making a move on her, she knew he wanted her. Just like she now wanted him. And maybe, just maybe, the self-made business mogul wanted her as much as she wanted him.

Because this? This relaxing in front of the TV? It was just for her.

Lysander's thumb brushed up along her neck and he traced her earlobe with the lightest caress of his fingertips. Rowan shivered.

"Cold?" Lysander asked.

She shook her head. "No."

"I would like to kiss you."

Rowan turned so their lips were only a breath apart. "I'd like that too."

His mouth pressed against hers softly. Once. Twice. Three times. Each touch of their lips teased and delighted in turn. She loved it. She wanted more. She wanted to taste him.

She initiated the next kiss, parting her lips just the littlest bit and exploring his mouth with hers. It was so good. The connection between their lips electrifying. Before she realized what was happening, her hands were buried in his dark hair as she tugged his head closer to hers, prolonging the kiss.

The tip of his tongue slid along her lips and she let hers meet it.

Her body felt like it was on fire, heat surging through her in volcanic waves.

Rowan wanted more. Not just more kissing, but touching. She climbed over Lysander so she was straddling his lap. Part of her brain was vaguely aware of him shifting so no pressure was on her hurt ankle. She ignored the tiny sting from the pressure she was putting on her knees.

This was too good to worry about minor discomfort.

His big hands cupped her bottom and kneaded, sending pleasure arcing through her. Their kiss became more intense as they explored each other's mouths and her breathing grew ragged.

His hands slid up her back until he reached the halter clasp on her dress. He stopped, breaking the kiss and panted. Then asked, "All right?"

"Yes," she said and dove back into the kiss.

The clasp came undone and then he was peeling the fabric down so her breasts were exposed. Her nipples were already hard, but now they tingled from being exposed to the air and she wanted oh so badly for him to touch her there.

Like he read her mind, Lysander brushed his palms over the turgid nubs, sending an arc of need directly to her core. It felt so good to be touched by another person, to know that person was as keen to touch her as she was to be touched. She arched her back, pressing her breasts into his hands, seeking more.

He gave it to her, gently squeezing the round globes in his hands and swiping his thumbs more firmly over her nipples.

She didn't know how long they kissed and touched each other, but at some point it just wasn't enough. She needed all of him, right now. Rowan broke the kiss and panted. Lysander's lips moved to her throat then down her chest.

She gasped as he sucked on the top of her breast. "More, Sander, I want more."

Tearing herself away from him, she shimmied out of her tiny dress and reveled in the look of approval and need he gave her. Then she put her fingers into either side of her panties and stopped. "You too. I want naked."

"*Ne.*" He said *yes,* slipping into Greek. She didn't mind. She was fluent and it showed how into the moment he was.

He stood and stripped with rapid movements, tossing his clothes to the floor. Rowan sucked in a breath of air, trying to move oxygen into her suddenly deprived lungs. Her soon to be lover was sculpted and bronze all over.

She licked her lips. "Do you sunbathe nude?"

"I swim laps in the morning."

"Without a suit."

"I like it better that way."

She nodded. She'd like it better that way if she were swimming with him too.

"The way you look at me is such a turn on," he said, his tone guttural.

She swallowed. "Same."

He looked at her like she was the sexiest thing he'd ever seen. Like airbrushed and botoxed wasn't perfection. She was.

They kissed again, their bodies pressing against each other, skin on skin. Every one of Rowan's nerve endings went zing. His body was hard all over, but the urgency of his need pressed into her stomach and she couldn't help wanting to touch him there. She grasped his hardon in her hand and slid up and down the impressive length.

Rowan wanted him inside her. She hoped he had condoms somewhere in this sanctuary of his.

When she'd decided to go through with this scheme, she'd gotten the birth control shot, but Lysander was sexually active, and she had no idea if he'd been tested recently. She wasn't taking any chances.

At least, that's what she told herself.

Chapter Six

Lysander maneuvered them to the sofa, and they spent glorious minutes exploring each other's bodies with hands and mouths.

At some point he grabbed a condom out of the first aid supplies.

Rowan laughed, even as relief washed over her. "You had Helen bring condoms with the bandages?"

"You said you wanted sex. I wanted to be prepared for whatever happened."

"I guess you've had sex outside the bedroom many times." He was too sexually confident to be limited by the standard location for intimacy.

Rowan, on the other hand, had never had sex anywhere but the marital bed. Her defunct marriage had not been a place to explore her sexually adventurous side.

"Yes," he agreed. He looked around them and then back at her. "It's the first time in here though. I don't usually bring lovers to my home and never in this room."

Right, because it was his inner sanctum.

She liked hearing that, but didn't make the mistake of saying so. They'd been very clear that they weren't dating. They were having sex. She had no claim on him, but still...she liked the sense that she was special.

"Let me," she said, taking the condom from him.

She opened the packet and then rolled the protection down his length, taking her time about it. Once she finished, she brushed up and down over the thin latex and reveled in how his body jerked in involuntary response to her touch.

He brushed her hands away. "Enough. You're going to make me come before I'm even inside you."

"Then I'd just have to entice you to hardness again, wouldn't I?" she asked without repentance.

The sound he made was pure sex.

Seconds later, she was under him, her thighs spread wide and his hardness pressing against the entrance to her body. "Ready?" he asked.

"Yes." More than.

He thrust with his hips, pushing himself inside her body. Sensation after sensation coursed through her as they found a rhythm that brought wave upon wave of ecstasy. Pleasure built from her core until she was tossing her head and canting her hips upward to meet every one of his thrusts.

He kissed her, his mouth passionate and desperate against her own before rearing up to change his angle slightly. He used one hand to steady himself, but the other was all over her, touching her breasts, her neck, her thigh, her stomach and finally sliding between them so his thumb could rub against her clitoris.

Rowan's climax took her by surprise, throwing her body into a rictus of ecstasy that did not end. Lysander kept moving, his handsome features set in stark lines of sexual need and then his head fell back and he shouted, his body going rigid above hers.

They moved together in aftershocks of joyous pleasure for long moments before he rolled to one side, pulling her into him as if unable to bear losing the physical connection.

He'd have to deal with the condom shortly, but right now, she let herself wallow in the aftermath of the most amazing sex she'd ever had. Her entire body tingled with lingering pleasure.

"I believe it is time to move to the bedroom."

"Oh, yes?" she asked, not really inclined to move at all.

"I want to bathe with you." His tone made the words an invitation to more pleasure.

"I've never bathed with someone before," she said thoughtfully. "It sounds fun."

"It will be," he promised.

He called for robes and they donned them before she followed him up a private staircase that led directly to his suite of rooms. The bedroom was large and decorated in dark wood, every piece of furniture substantial, including the bed that looked like a family of five could easily sleep in it.

But they hadn't come up for the bed, no matter how decadent, as evidenced by him walking directly into the ensuite. She followed without hesitation, but stopped when she saw the large whirlpool tub that dominated one corner of the bathroom as big as the bedroom in her current apartment.

"Wow." Steaming water was already bubbling away. "Did you have Helen run us a bath?"

She wasn't going to be embarrassed by that. She wasn't. She was a grown woman who had decided to have sex with the one man she wanted. She had nothing to be embarrassed of.

"Her, or one of her minions." He shrugged. "I sent the text to her."

Amused, Rowan smiled. "She has minions?"

"In a house this size? She has a full staff at her beck and call."

"I bet every one of them adores her."

"They do. She's a good employer."

"But aren't you their employer?"

"I pay them, but she has full discretion for hiring and firing."

"You trust her a great deal."

"My mother hired her."

She loved that he trusted his mother that much. "I'm surprised your mom doesn't live here with you."

"I'm well past the age of living with my mother and she is not who I want to think about right now."

Rowan found herself grinning. She played teasingly with the tie on her robe. "I wonder who exactly you would rather be thinking about."

"I think you know," he said with a mock growl and then he was helping her with that pesky tie and leading her to the bubbling tub.

Rowan learned that waterproof lube made lovemaking in the bath much easier and a lot of fun. She also learned that as intense as Lysander could be, he liked to laugh, and intimacy felt even more intimate when that laughter was shared.

~ ~ ~

They ate dinner in their robes on the balcony, though there was a temporary wardrobe rack filled with clothes in Rowan's style, preferred colors and size. When he opted for a robe, rather than dressing, so did she.

Rowan enjoyed the privacy of eating the delicious moussaka and salad on the balcony with Lysander her only companion. They talked about everything from the road works projects in Athens to her desire to go parasailing.

"You've never gone? But why not?" he asked.

Rowan savored a bite of salad before answering. She loved olives and feta in her salad and Lysander's chef mixed a dressing that had just the right balance of tangy vinegar, olive oil and herbs.

"My ex strongly discouraged me from wearing a swimsuit in public," she said after swallowing all that yumminess.

One of the things she missed sometimes about the life she'd left behind was never having to prepare her own food. She was learning to cook though, and it wasn't going too badly. She'd burned a few things, and over salted others, but all-in-all, Rowan thought she was getting the hang of it. She couldn't make anything like this meal though.

Her one and only attempt at moussaka had turned out more like a soup than a casserole.

Lysander's brows drew together, a storm brewing in his dark eyes. "I know Cyrus is a fool, but why not?"

"He wasn't enamored of my body." He'd been embarrassed by her, or at least that was what his words and actions implied.

Rowan had thanked the powers that be more than once that she'd fallen in love with a phantom and not the real man. Yes, Cyrus's attitude had hurt, more in the beginning than the end of their marriage. But once Rowan had realized he'd played a part to woo her into marriage and that the real Cyrus was selfish and lacking in both empathy and compassion, she'd stopped giving his opinions much weight at all.

And that had been before she'd found out he'd been cheating on her since before they even said, "I do."

"So?" Lysander asked with the dismissiveness he always directed toward his half-brother. "Why should that stop you trying something you wanted to?"

"It's not going to now," she said with a shrug. "I'll probably even go on the cruise to Mexico I've always wanted to. I may even combine the two."

"You want to go...on a cruise?" he asked, like the idea was beyond his comprehension.

She stifled a giggle at the look of horror he couldn't quite hide. "Oh, yes. I've always wanted to."

"But Cyrus has a yacht. Surely you spent time sailing on it."

"It's not the same. Whenever we traveled it was with his friends and business associates. Cruise ships are full of strangers, interesting people I can get to know and lots of things to do." She'd found the views the only redeeming element to otherwise nearly unbearably boring trips aboard her ex-husband's yacht.

"You want to meet strangers?" This time the horror was right there for her to see and hear.

She couldn't help laughing. "You sound like you wonder if I'm using all my brain cells."

"I would never imply otherwise," he said quickly, but his expression didn't match his words.

Even as she felt a little bubble of warmth at this indication that though he could be a cranky so-and-so with other people, he was trying to be careful of *her* feelings, Rowan burst out giggling again and shook her head. "There's world class chefs providing the food, nightly entertainment, decks you can hang out on."

"But you have all of that on a yacht."

"Didn't you ever watch *The Love Boat* as a kid?"

"No. What is it?"

"It was a show in the 1970s."

"You weren't even born then."

"Syndication," she replied with a roll of her eyes. "People fell in love on board and there was a cruise director who made sure everyone had fun, and a bartender who was a real chick magnet."

"And this made you want to take a cruise?" he asked doubtfully. "You do realize real life is not like television. Especially television from many decades ago."

She shrugged, not bothered he didn't share her vision. She wasn't asking him to come with her. She would find a friend to share a cabin and go on her cruise. Someday.

"Why Mexico?" he asked. "You do realize where we live?"

The look on his face. The general bewilderment in his tone. She had to stifle a giggle. He really did look perplexed.

Lysander Baros was Greek, through and through. The idea of wanting to soak in the sun on any sea but those surrounding his beloved country was beyond his comprehension.

Oh, he was well traveled and sophisticated in his tastes as only a man who had eaten food from the best chefs in most of the world's largest cities could be. But that travel? Those meals? They had mostly been to further his business interests.

Maybe the idea of taking a vacation, of traveling simply for the sake of enjoyment was as baffling to him as where she wanted to go.

Poor, driven tycoon.

She'd thought about a cruise on the Mediterranean, but as much as she loved the beauty and people of her adopted country, she wanted to experience something entirely different. "I have lived in Greece for the past ten years. I want to go somewhere I have never been."

"Your parents never took you to Mexico?"

"No. When we traveled, we came to Europe." Her parents had considered places like Paris, Rome, and London worthy destinations.

And of course Athens, where her father had worked so hard to build business relations with Lysander's father.

"I love the colorfulness of Mexico, the way the Mexican language is different from Spanish in other countries, especially Spain." She had taken Spanish in high school and been taught by a woman from Mexico. Rowan's teacher had been very clear on the differences. "I want to learn more about the country, its culture and its people."

"I'm not sure a cruise is your best way to do that."

Could he sound any more condescending?

"There are shore excursions. I'll get a little taste of lots of places." And she would do tons of reading before her cruise. She loved learning new things.

"More like a taste of the tourist areas."

"That's as valid an experience as anything else," she insisted.

"But hardly the authentic Mexico."

"First of all, Mexico is a whole country, so no one city is authentic to all of it. Second of all, you're probably right, but I still want to do it."

He just looked at her, his dark eyes asking why?

"I'm sure that the days I spend on shore will give me an idea for where I'd like to come when I return to Mexico for a hopefully longer visit." She smiled, thinking about the prospect.

Maybe she would use just a tiny bit of her divorce settlement for travel.

She could still do a lot of good with what was left over.

"The point of the cruise isn't just the shore excursions or getting to visit another country." Rowan was also excited about what she expected life onboard to be like.

It was the experience on the ship. Getting to know the other passengers. Meeting people from all walks of life. Playing shuffleboard. Did they still play shuffleboard on cruises? She'd find out. Some day.

"You're a very unique woman." He didn't sound judgy now. In fact, he was almost admiring.

"I don't think so. Lots of people go on cruises and even more dream about it." Maybe just not people as wealthy and driven as Lysander.

"But few of them have access to a private yacht and the Mediterranean."

"I *had* access to a yacht during my marriage. I don't anymore." Her family had never had a yacht. Her parents had borrowed Cyrus's a couple of times every year. She wondered if they had last year, while she'd been fighting the legal battle for her divorce?

"Do you want access to a yacht?" he asked.

Was he offering his? "No. I told you; I want to go on a cruise."

He shook his head, like he couldn't quite believe what he was hearing. "To Mexico."

"Exactly."

Chapter Seven

The next morning, Rowan woke beside Lysander, her body still lethargic from the surfeit of pleasure their night together had brought. She didn't want to leave the warmth of his body, much less his bed, but they'd set the parameters very succinctly. No commitments. Just sex. Not feelings.

Rowan frowned, her heart squeezing a little in her chest. It wasn't a great time to realize she might be one of those people for whom sex was never just a physical act. Even married to a man she'd rapidly fallen out of love with, she'd felt an emotional connection to him because of the sex they shared, no matter how infrequent.

Which was why she'd been so hurt to find out about his infidelity. She hadn't loved him any longer, but that act of sex between them? It had still felt like something important, something he should not have been doing with other people while married to her.

However, what she'd experienced last night with Lysander blew ten years of tepid emotional connection out of the water. Every time she'd taken Lysander into her body, she'd felt like their souls collided and entwined.

And hers felt bruised this morning from all the mental reminders she'd had to give herself not to settle into the feelings.

They weren't real.

It was just sex. Amazing, mind blowing, never before experienced emotionally intense sex. At least for her. But still, it had only been a temporary pleasure. Nothing lasting.

Lysander didn't do commitment and did Rowan really want one? Regardless of how incredible the night before had been, how connected she had felt to her Greek billionaire lover, she didn't want strings that tethered her to a life that wasn't hers to lead as she saw fit.

After losing ten years of her life to a bad marriage, Rowan wanted to experience all the adventures life had to offer. She was never going back into the wife-of-an-important-businessman box again, that jail cell that only allowed for certain behaviors and certain friends.

She'd always bucked against the constraints, but her efforts had been thwarted by both her husband's and her own family's expectations. She'd wanted to take a paid, fulltime position with her organization from the beginning. Cyrus had allowed part-time volunteer work. Looking back, she hated that she'd agreed to keep the peace.

She'd made friends that didn't further her husband's or father's business interests, but the time she'd had to spend with them had been minimal. She'd been used to juggling the life she wanted with the life she led. She'd been doing it since she was a child, being encouraged by her mother to invite certain children home to play.

At some point that juggling had felt more like trying to catch spinning plates in the air. Rowan had been so stifled in those last couple of years, it had been hard to breathe.

So, she needed to get out of this bed, get dressed and get the heck out of Lysander's house. They'd had their fun, now it was time for her to go.

Moving very carefully, so as not to wake him, she slid toward the side of the bed.

"Where are you going?"

Rowan startled and turned quickly to face him. "Um, it's morning."

"I am aware. We didn't close the curtains to the balcony," he said.

Right. The sun shone into the room brightly, though it had risen only a little while before.

"I should get going."

"Why? You do not have to work. Today is Saturday. You have clothing here for any eventuality we may plan."

"That wardrobe hanger is pretty full. Why is that?" Had he planned on her staying the weekend? Was that what he wanted?

Was that what *she* wanted?

"I am thorough."

"We agreed to one night."

"Did we?" he asked.

"You said you don't do commitment."

"Are you saying you got enough?"

She stared at him, pretty sure she could never make that particular claim. "What are you saying?"

"Your intention was to get the message through to Cyrus that your marriage is over. One night *might* do it, but a full-on affair? That would *definitely* get the point across."

"You want to be my lover long term to stick it to your half-brother?"

"I want to be your lover, for whatever term, because last night was not enough for me. Was it for you?" The demand she answer the question this time was in his tone, but his face was neutral.

"No."

"Yet, you were leaving."

Seriously? He was stuck on that. "That was the agreement."

"When you make a deal, you stick to it." No question how he felt about that. He approved. It was in his tone, but also the warmth of his gaze left no doubt.

"I do."

"Make a deal with me now. We are lovers for as long as we both want to be."

"Okay." She could live with that. More than. Though she didn't know how her heart was going to handle the inevitable breakup. That was a problem for the future. Today, she was going to live the life she wanted to and that included being Lysander's lover.

She sat up and tugged the bedding with her to cover her naked breasts. "But if either of us decides we want to see other people, we tell the other *before* a date, or anything else."

She didn't want to feature as the cheated-on girlfriend in the tabloids any more than she'd enjoyed being featured as the betrayed wife in the many salacious articles detailing Cyrus's bedroom behavior. She'd first learned of his infidelity through a friend who'd seen one such article.

When confronted, Cyrus had dismissed the article as journalism at its basest at first, claiming the pictures were photoshopped.

Her mom had been the one to finally confirm Rowan's suspicions. Calling her to give her a *pep talk* about how men and women saw marriage differently and that she couldn't take Cyrus's affairs personally. Coming from a woman who had consistently turned a blind eye to her own husband's indiscretions, the words had carried more weight than the tabloid article.

Cyrus had been unfaithful, and Rowan's mother knew it. Had, as Rowan learned later, known all along.

"Agreed."

"That included your friends with benefits thing with Adele Fournier." He wasn't getting any other *benefits* while he was sharing Rowan's bed.

"I told you. While I am in a liaison with one woman, I do not have sex with others." He tugged at the sheet covering her. "Now, since we are both awake, let us make better use of our time than talking."

And they did.

The next two days were idyllic for Rowan. Lysander was an inventive and eager lover. She learned a lot about her own body's responses she'd never known. His personal shopper had excellent taste and Rowan felt no urge to return to her apartment before she absolutely had to.

That was Sunday night.

Only Lysander wasn't keen on her leaving.

~ ~ ~

"Why can't you go to work from here in the morning?" Lysander asked Rowan. He liked having her in his home and the sex was something outside his experience.

He liked sex. It was both pleasure and stress relief. What was not to like? But with Rowan, it was more. It was fun. And he wanted her all the time. Like now.

She stood there in a pair of jeans and a top that hugged her generous curves, looking like she didn't understand the question and all he wanted to do was strip those clothes off her and start touching.

"Lysander, we've spent the entire weekend together and if I know you, you'll be up and out of bed hours before I am." She sounded reasonable.

He didn't want practical. He wanted her, in his bed every night until they burned out this conflagration of desire between them. "We'll have the night together," he pointed out, not sure why he had to.

Surely, that was obvious.

"More sex?" she asked, sounding surprised. "I've never had so much sex in a week, maybe even a month, much less a weekend."

He liked hearing that. Which was strange. Although he expected monogamy during his temporary liaisons, he was not a possessive lover. However, with Rowan, all his atavistic instincts were kicking in.

"Probably." He grinned at her, feeling...happy. That was not usually a word he used to describe himself.

Driven. Focused. Determined. All those and more, but happy? It was odd. He liked it, though.

She gave him an assessing look. "You're way less grumpy than I remember."

"I am not grumpy," he said, feeling offended. He wasn't antisocial, just not overly friendly. It was necessary to maintain a certain distance from others.

"You hardly ever smile. That first time we danced, I thought you were angry at me."

"I was not angry with you." He'd been furious to learn she was married to his estranged half-brother.

Lysander had been attracted to Rowan from the first moment he saw her luscious curves in no way diminished by her designer gown's attempt at modesty. She was beautiful, and everything he found sexually appealing in a woman, but she'd been married.

That she was tied to his selfish prick of a sibling only made it worse.

"Oh, I figured that out. Cyrus was mad, but I figured out that you pretty much frown at everybody."

"I do not frown at everyone. A lack of a smile is not de facto a frown. My most common expression is neutral boredom." At least when surrounded by people like his father and brother.

Lysander did not enjoy superficial and made no attempt to pretend he did.

"Um, if you say so, but you have to admit that you don't bother with polite conversation either."

He shrugged. "When a man with my wealth and influence smiles at someone, they take it as an invitation to make an approach."

Could he sound more pretentious? But what he said was true.

"And that's a bad thing?" she asked.

"They almost always ask for something. Usually money."

"The price of success, I guess. I'll probably hit you up for a donation for the foundation I work for too sometime."

Why didn't that bother him? Because she was so open about it? Or just because it was her?

"Anyway, I'm sure some people just want a chance to talk to you. You're like a celebrity." Her tone was teasing.

So, he ignored the celebrity remark. "I have no time for small talk."

She laughed softly, like he'd been joking. He wasn't.

"My father and Cyrus excel at discussing golf, stock prices and the next big thing. They smile a lot too," she said, like she was thinking about that and wasn't sure what she thought.

"And that signifies what?" Lysander asked. "Both are men that would approach me for business capital with the least encouragement. Even my half-brother, who refuses to speak to me otherwise, would leverage our tenuous family ties if he thought he had a chance of sharing in a business venture."

Regardless of how they liked to be seen, neither man approached Lysander's wealth or power in the business world. When he'd been younger, he'd had nothing compared to them, but now? He could buy either man several times over. He didn't say that because he didn't think the tender-hearted Rowan would appreciate it.

"You really wouldn't do a business deal with Cyrus?" she asked. "I always thought that was all in his head. You don't go out of your way to be rude to him."

Not like his brother, she meant. Cyrus got his petty thrills from making it obvious that though their father acknowledged Lysander as a son, Cyrus would never acknowledge him as a brother. He was sure the other man regretted taking that stance now, but he was too entrenched in it to backtrack without losing major face.

"No," he said in answer to Rowan's question. "I choose my business partners carefully." And his brother was not a good bet.

For many more reasons than the family drama.

"Not too carefully, or you wouldn't have had to sever ties with a company that has connections to an organization that thinks threatening you will get you to back off on your clean energy stance," Rowan pointed out with sass.

Lysander frowned, not enjoying this reminder of his fallibility, despite how charming he found her teasing. "That was an unfortunate oversight on the part of one of my upper managers."

Rowan's eyes widened. "Does he still have a job?"

"Yes, but he has been demoted and placed under the mentorship of a director I know I can trust." The remaining acquisition managers had been required to do additional training in asset assessment as well.

Lysander wasn't risking the same thing ever happening again.

"You thought you could trust this man."

Lysander shrugged. "I don't pretend to be perfect."

Something shifted in Rowan's gaze, almost like she admired him all the more for having made an error in judgment. She didn't react like other people, and he liked that about her.

"No. You don't pretend anything," she said with satisfaction. "But there are a lot of tycoon level businesspeople who think they can do no wrong. It's nice knowing you can acknowledge your mistakes."

"If we cannot learn from our errors, we cannot grow." No matter how good a person was at something, there would always be those moments when they fumbled. "For the sake of my employees and shareholders, I try to manage the risk so mine are not catastrophic."

Her eyes shone with approval that he was fast growing addicted to. "I love that you included your employees in that statement."

"Of course I do. The people I employ are why I am where I am."

"I don't think many billionaires would say that. I know a few millionaires who definitely wouldn't."

She was talking about her father and Cyrus. "You cannot judge all businessmen by your father and my half-brother."

"I'm not. I've been around men like my father my whole life."

"And still you married Cyrus."

"We're doing this now?" she asked.

Chapter Eight

"It appears we are." He had a hard time understanding how a woman like her had ended up with a waste of space like Cyrus.

"My parents coached him on how to win me over. I didn't know they were feeding him intel on my likes and dislikes. I'm still not sure why everyone was so vested in me marrying Cyrus, but even my older brother got in on it."

His own father would have no qualms about betraying his own child in the same way. Lysander's mother, on the other hand, would sooner kill a user like Cyrus than help him marry her daughter.

Lysander had no siblings, but he knew his mother would have done her best to protect her daughter, just as she had him.

"How did you find out?"

"After we'd been married a while, I pushed Cyrus to explain why he'd changed so much. It was one of our rare fights, not because we agreed on all things but because we didn't have a relationship in which open and honest discussion was encouraged. Anyway, he let it slip that he'd done what he had to make me fall in love with him."

"You stayed."

"I did, but my love died when I realized that the man I thought I loved didn't exist and never had."

"And still you stayed."

"I made promises."

"And then you found out he'd broken his."

"Yes."

"You're very old world in some ways."

"If you're saying that I believe in justice and that him having a plethora of lovers while married to me was justification for divorcing him, you're right."

"Yes, that is what I was saying." But he stood by the way he'd said it. She had a way of looking at the world that reminded him of a medieval knight.

Her honor mattered to her, but so did the integrity of the people she'd sworn her allegiance to. He wanted to be one of those people.

She smiled brightly at him, the warmth in her gaze doing something strange in the area of his heart. "You're kind of amazing, do you know that?"

"Does that mean you are spending the night with this amazing man?" he asked as he pulled her into his arms like he'd been wanting to do since she started making noises about going back to her apartment.

"Hmm..." she said, tilting her head and exaggerating a thoughtful expression. "There's my empty apartment where chores that I usually spend the entire weekend taking care of are waiting to be done before bed."

"Yes?"

"And there's you."

"And there is me." He couldn't help it. He kissed her.

When he lifted his head, her expression was hazy, but she was still smiling. "You win. You definitely win. I mean laundry doesn't feel all that urgent when I still have a week's worth of new outfits I've never worn, courtesy of my very generous lover."

"An investment in clothing has never been so well spent, then."

She reached up and kissed him. "You are so not the grumpy guy everyone thinks."

"I am not a grumpy guy at all."

She just laughed, like that was funny. But he was being serious. He wasn't bad tempered. Was he? What would his mother say? He knew what she'd say when she found out he was dating Rowan. She was going to be over the moon.

She lived with the perpetual hope he would marry one day and give her grandchildren. He never told her how unlikely that event was. He did not want to break her heart.

"I know you planned to call in the paparazzi for your *morning after* walk," he said. "However, I wonder if it might be more pleasant to announce our status as a couple by attending the Vasileiou Gala."

The look on her face made it clear Rowan had completely forgotten about calling the paparazzi to catch her leaving Lysander's house after staying the night. He, on the other hand, rarely forgot anything.

"I think you might be right about him wanting me back for reasons other than sheer bloody-mindedness, so I'm not sure it matters if he knows we're together, but that doesn't stop me wanting to go to the gala with you."

He liked hearing that. Liked it a lot that she made it clear spending time with him was what was important, not her plan to turn Cyrus off her.

Lysander liked that plan though and had his own ideas of how to make it happen. He did need a look at her prenuptial agreement though. He thought it might take some business acumen rather than just showing Cyrus that Rowan had moved on. Lysander had to admit that he didn't mind that bit either.

She'd been right about one thing. Though it was nowhere near the top reason he wanted to take her to the gala, rubbing his half-brother's face in the fact that Rowan was with Lysander now had a great deal of appeal. If for no other reason than to show Cyrus what an idiot he'd been to treat his marriage with so little consideration.

The Vasileiou Gala would work very well as an opportunity to let Athens society know Lysander and Rowan were seeing each other.

Lysander found he liked the thought of that. He and Cyrus had little in common, including the charities they supported. With one exception. This one. In fact, he'd seen Rowan for the first time at that year's Vasileiou Gala. He'd asked her to dance and he'd been charmed by her. He had also been turned on. Then he'd learned she was married to his brother.

Oh, yeah, Lysander could be certain his half-brother would be at the gala. It was such a high-profile event, the Andino family never missed it.

Cyrus would get the memo about Lysander and Rowan all right.

So would their father, which would probably have more effect on cooling Cyrus's enthusiasm for trying to get back together with his ex-wife. Cyrus didn't take being shown up well. Knowing Rowan was with Lysander would irk the other man, but having the rest of the world know it? Would make her radioactive where Cyrus was concerned.

Rowan had been right that if she was seen leaving Lysander's house *the morning after*, it would nix Cyrus's desire for reconciliation. Provided that desire was motivated by possessiveness, or even some type of affection. However, Lysander was not convinced that it was. He needed to get a look at her prenup and maybe do some digging into holdings she might not even realize were in her name.

"Does it bother you seeing your father with his wife?" Rowan asked, interrupting his thoughts.

Lysander frowned. His father had presented the image of solidly married man, with his wife on his arm at every public event for Lysander's entire life. That couldn't be what Rowan meant. "His current wife, you mean?"

Rowan nodded.

"That's a heavy question for me, are you sure you want the answer?" he said, being more candid than he would have been with anyone else, except his mother.

"Yes." Rowan pressed in closer to him. "I want to know everything about you."

Why did hearing that make him want to smile. Their liaison was temporary. He had to admit, if only to himself, he was just as curious about her. "The short answer is no."

"And the long answer?" she prompted.

"It bothered the hell out of me that he did not marry my mother when his first wife died, but it did not surprise me." Lysander was too pragmatic not to have realized a long time ago what a shallow human being Baptiste Andino was.

Citing adherence to his religious beliefs that did not allow for divorce, Lysander's father had kept his mother on a string, living as his mistress, for decades while remaining married to the socialite wife with all the right connections. When the first Mrs. Andino had died three years before, Lysander's father had started dating a bare six months after he buried her. And he'd married another socialite whose family had business connections he wanted a year later.

The fact she was twenty years younger and considered beautiful had no doubt played their role as well, Lysander thought cynically. His father was all about the image.

His loyal, trusting mother had never even been in the running, despite the fact that Baptiste recognized Lysander as his.

"A man of his ilk does not marry his mistress," Lysander said.

It had devastated his mother when she'd realized all the promises and if-only-I-wasn't-married refrains she'd heard from the man were nothing but hot air, but it had been the best thing that could have happened to her too. At least as far as Lysander could see.

It had never been Baptiste's religious conviction that kept him married, no matter what he'd told the woman who had born him his second son. It had been pure self-interest. Just as self-interest had prompted Baptiste's second marriage to *someone suitable*.

Lysander's mother had finally broken things off with his father the night he announced his engagement to his current wife. Lysander had been so proud of her, even as he'd held her while she cried.

He'd vowed in that moment never to cause a woman that kind of heartache. Lysander would never make vows he could not keep.

He would never have more than one lover at a time, but he would not make promises to any of them. He didn't do forever, wasn't sure it was even possible.

Chapter Nine

"You don't think much of him, do you?" Rowan asked perceptively.

"No. Do you?" he asked. "You lived in the same house with him for years. You probably know him better than I do, despite me being his son."

Rowan's lovely features twisted with distaste. "No, I never did think much of him. He didn't even try to be discreet about his affairs. I guess that's one reason why finding out Cyrus was a philanderer came as such a shock."

"Because he was better at hiding it."

"Yes. I think modern sensibilities are less forgiving of that sort of thing. When your father was a young man, it was common for powerful men to have what they called their *pillow friends*."

Lysander hated thinking of his mother in those terms, but she'd never been anything else to Baptiste. Even the house Lysander had grown up in had not belonged to her. A mistress didn't own her home, she lived at the behest of her lover and provider.

"Culture swings on a pendulum." At least on the surface.

Lysander wasn't sure there were any fewer men of his standing that took lovers, but they weren't as forthright about it. It all sickened him. His mother's life, his own life, could have been so different if his father had been a man who kept his word.

"What put that look on your face?" Rowan asked.

Lysander shook his head before moving to take her hand and tug her out of the room and toward the stairs.

"Where are we going?" she asked with laughter in her voice.

"Where do you think?" he riposted.

More laughter was his only answer.

When they reached his bedroom and he'd shut the door on the rest of the world, Lysander shocked himself by saying, "My father paid for my schooling. He paid for our lifestyle, but the car she drove belonged to him. The house she raised me in was his. One of the first things I did when I reached my initial financial goal was to buy my mother a house and a car that were in her name."

"You wanted her to be independent."

"I wanted her to leave my father, but that didn't come until later." As had his mother's move into the house he'd bought for her.

"He must have loved her, in his way," Rowan said. "He stayed in a relationship with her for longer than a lot of marriages last."

"While remaining married to another woman."

"Yes, but I saw him after Iona broke up with him. I'm pretty sure it happened the night he announced his engagement to his current wife. He was all smiles at the engagement party, but the next morning he was haggard, like he'd aged ten years in a night."

Lysander had never thought his father would grieve the breakup. "It was probably something else."

"No, I don't think it was. He used to slip and call his new wife Iona. He did the same thing to my mother-in-law when she was alive. I don't know if he still does it as I haven't seen him with her in over a year."

Lysander shrugged. "I wouldn't know." He rarely saw his father and almost never in the company of his wife.

Still, something shifted in Lysander's chest at the knowledge that his mother breaking things off had affected his father so badly. Regardless, the man had been selfish and manipulative in his relationship with Lysander's mother and Lysander would never forget the pain she'd suffered because of it.

"Enough about my father," Lysander said. "It is you I'm focused on right now."

"Oh, yes?" Rowan walked across Lysander's sitting room and opened the doors leading to the balcony. She stopped only when she stood at the chest high wall surrounding the balcony and took in a deep breath. "I love the privacy here. We're outside but no one can see us."

"Only the birds," he agreed. It was one of the reasons the wall was so high, privacy and safety. "There are no good angles for the paparazzi no matter how good their camera's zoom lens."

"Not unless they can fly." She turned to face him, her hands on the hem of her top. "We can do anything we want and no one can see us," she repeated.

Then she pulled her top off over her head, leaving her in hip hugging jeans and a lacy bra that put her luscious curves on display.

All melancholy inevitably brought on by thoughts of his parents' relationship were swept away by the tsunami of lust that slammed through his body. He went painfully erect in a matter of seconds, which no matter what people wanted to believe was not the norm. Not even for a viral man in his prime like Lysander.

But she affected him as no other woman ever had.

Rowan's lips curved in a come-hither smile. "Like what you see?"

"I wouldn't mind seeing more," he said.

"Like this?" She reached behind herself and suddenly her bra was sliding down her arms and her generous breasts were spilling out.

Wanting to cup them in his hands he took an involuntary step forward. His mouth watered with the desire to suck on her nipples. The little noises of passion she made when he did were one of his new favorite things.

But he couldn't move any further than that half step. He was frozen into immobility by his reaction to her. He was so hard, it hurt to have himself confined in his slacks.

Rowan's beauty was Rubenesque, not conventional. Her tummy had a little curve he loved to caress, her thighs and butt were lush and he was addicted to every inch of her.

"It hardly seems fair for me to be the only one undressing," she teased pointedly.

He agreed, but his legs were still locked. Finally, Lysander managed to pull his polo style shirt over his head before tossing it to the floor.

The setting sun turned Rowan's body golden as she unzipped and wiggled out of her jeans, leaving her in only a pair of panties. Since she could have taken them off with the jeans, she'd left them on with a purpose.

To tease him.

And tease him, they did.

He wanted to see the copper curls nestled in the apex between her thighs. His mouth salivated with the desire to taste her there.

"You make me burn with that look in your eyes," she said huskily.

He had to swallow before he could speak. "Fair. You make me burn just being in the same room."

She expelled a soft sigh. "I don't care if you say the same thing to all the women you sleep with, I like hearing it."

"You're the only one."

Cupping her own breasts, like she was offering them to him for his pleasure, she smiled. "Even better."

Making a primal sound he'd never heard from himself before taking this woman to his bed, Lysander stripped out of the rest of his clothes with lightning speed. Then he crossed the few feet that separated them and pulled her against his body.

Her arms came up and landed on his shoulders, her pillowy breasts pressing into his chest. "I thought maybe you were going to stand there and look at me for the rest of the night."

"No chance." Not when touching and tasting were in the offing.

Her laughter went straight to his dick, succeeding in the impossible...making him even harder. This is what she did to him. Every time.

Even before her divorce, she'd turned him on. Lysander had avoided her because she was so completely off limits, but now she was *his* lover. He reveled in the ability to slide his hands down Rowan's silky back and over her curved bottom. His hips thrust forward of their own volition rubbing his erection against her stomach.

She gave a throaty purr and he was lost.

Lysander picked her up so their sexes could kiss and she helped him, spreading her legs and hooking them around his hips. They kissed, eating at each other's mouths, her moans vibrating against his lips and his hardon pressing against the silk barrier of her panties.

She broke from the kiss. "I want you, Sander!"

He didn't bother to respond with words, but lowered her so she was once again standing. Then he dropped to his knees and slid her panties down her legs. The scent of her arousal perfumed the air around them.

Pressing her legs further apart, he shifted forward and tasted her.

She cried out and leaned back against the stone wall of the balcony.

There was something so decadent and primal about making love outside. The balcony gave them complete privacy, but the air brushed their skin like another lover's caress.

He pleasured her with his tongue and fingers, sliding one into her slick, hot entrance. He pressed up and rubbed on that spot that sent her into raptures. She squirmed, her legs buckling, and he held her up while he tasted her sweet nectar.

"Please, Sander..." she moaned out. "I need you inside me."

Swiping at his face with the back of his hand, he stood and gave her exactly what she was asking for, thrusting inside her with unerring accuracy honed over the multiple times they'd made love in the last two days.

Her silky flesh gripped his cock tightly as he pushed deeper into her soaked depths.

Lysander was grateful she'd told him after their first time that she was on birth control. He'd shown her his health results and told her he hadn't had a lover since the tests. She'd had hers on her phone and insisted on doing the same before agreeing to forego the condom.

He'd realized he didn't need to see her test results to believe her though.

He trusted Rowan like he never trusted anyone. Lysander knew deep in his gut that she would never lie to him.

Their bodies locked together, he took her mouth in a breath stealing kiss just in time to stifle her scream. Rowan was a noisy lover.

And that turned him on more than he thought it could.

They moved together for long moments, but as much pleasure as this joining afforded, he couldn't get the angle he wanted. Rowan seemed frustrated as well, breaking from the kiss to shake her head and moan.

"Try a different position?" he asked, his voice just above a growl.

"Yes. *Something*. I'm so close."

He disentangled their bodies and turned hers, so she faced the balcony. "Lean on the wall."

She did, arching her back and thrusting her behind toward him. It was all the invitation he needed, and he entered her from behind, sliding back into silky smooth, welcoming heat. He reached around and cupped her breast with one of his hands, lightly pinching the hard nipple while sliding his other hand down her body until he could press his middle finger against her clitoris.

She moaned, canting her hips forward and then arching back as if she couldn't decide what stimulation she needed more. His dick deep inside her, or the press of his finger against her sensitive bundle of nerves.

Lysander alternated between making circles around her clit and sliding directly over it with his fingertip until she was panting and pleading for more. He continued to touch her in the way she'd shown him she liked, driving her closer and closer to orgasm.

Increasing the pace, he drove into her with hard thrusts until she went rigid under him and cried out her release. Her vaginal walls contracted like a vice around his sex pulling him even deeper into her body and making him come. His shout joined hers and Lysander didn't care if everyone on staff could hear them.

This was so damn good.

Perfect.

They were both sweaty and heaving after, but he sat on the L shaped outdoor sofa and pulled her naked into his lap, running his hands over her body as their breathing slowly returned to normal.

This lazy touching was another of his new favorite things. He found Rowan's luscious curves addicting.

~ ~ ~

Rowan nestled into Lysander's arms, enjoying the soft glide of his big hands over her body. He made no effort to hide how much he relished touching her and she loved that. There was no one upmanship when she was in bed with Lysander.

He didn't make a big deal about who came first, but he always made sure that they both did. He didn't ask her how it was, maybe because it was always so obvious that it had been very, very satisfying.

For both of them.

Best of all, Lysander never critiqued her *performance* and told her what she could do to make it better in the future. Her ex had done that. It had hurt her at first, and then just annoyed her. Sex wasn't a job Rowan performed.

It was an experience between two people, both of them equally responsible for how it went.

It was that way with Lysander. He paid attention to her responses and listened when she said anything. Like earlier, changing their angle. What they'd been doing had felt so hot, but she'd hung on the edge of that precipice of pleasure and wanted to soar right over.

He'd listened and then they'd both gotten what they needed.

"I like this," she said, kissing his neck before she laid her head against his shoulder.

"I do too."

She knew he did. The languid touching afterward usually led to another bout of lovemaking, and she doubted this time would be any different. Sex had never been so consuming for her, and she had thought it was a myth that men could do it more than once in a night.

Apparently, it wasn't, and she was the lucky recipient of repeated proof of that.

CHAPTER TEN

The next morning, Klaus brought Rowan's car to the front of the villa. Lysander was already in a meeting, though he'd offered to have her driven to work and picked up afterward. This time, she'd stood firm on her plan to return to her apartment. She was a grownup with things that needed tending.

Only later that evening as she let herself into the silent and empty place, she had to try hard to remember what they were and why they were so important. If she'd gone back to Lysander's, they'd be sharing a drink before dinner and she'd be looking forward to another night of amazing lovemaking.

No matter how tantalizing, that wasn't her life. Rowan had spent years living in a loveless marriage because it had been what was expected of her. She'd had every creature comfort seen to, but her soul had starved. Well, her soul wasn't starving anymore. She thrived working full-time for an organization she believed in. The only constraint on her time with the friends of her choosing were the things she had committed to doing, not things committed to on her behalf.

Not that her family hadn't tried. Rowan's mom had expected her to move back into the family home and do what she'd always done, support her father's business interests. Of course, she'd expected Rowan to stay married to Cyrus too. Neither were going to happen.

She'd gone back to the States, but only temporarily, so she could start divorce proceedings. She'd returned for the necessary arbitration and hearing, but her life was in Greece now and that was where it would stay.

Rowan hadn't walked away from Cyrus only to move back into the same constricting existence with her parents. In the last two years, she'd worked hard to make a life for herself, one that she could be proud to live. One that fed her soul.

And that was why she was here, making a sandwich for dinner, instead of dining with Lysander in five-star splendor, she reminded herself. After starting a load of laundry, she started going through the mail that had piled up in her absence. How was it that there was still so much physical mail when almost all of her bills were paid online and no one ever sent her any letters?

Although most of the mail was simply junk destined for the recycling bin, a few things were invitations to events her parents would expect her to attend. For the sake of maintaining some semblance of a relationship with them, she would say yes to at least one.

Although invitations were handled via email and social media among her chosen friends, certain organizations that catered to the wealthy elite still insisted on printed invites with RSVP cards and their embossed return envelopes. It was a matter of fulfilling expectations.

Rowan considered consulting with Lysander before choosing the invitation to say yes to. If he was already planning to go, then if it worked for her schedule, she'd prefer to RSVP a yes to that event. She wasn't kidding herself though. She knew he worked long hours and if she wanted to see him during whatever time they chose to remain lovers, she had to be creative about making that happen.

She might even have to accommodate, but unlike every year until she'd walked out on her ex, Rowan wasn't going to be the only one doing the accommodating. Lysander would have to make time for them in his schedule or they wouldn't last very long. No matter how mind blowing the sex was.

He'd already taken an entire weekend to spend with her and though she knew he liked his decompress time when he returned from a trip, she'd heard him giving instructions to reschedule some calls and a dinner meeting the night before with some consortium out of Belgium.

Rowan grabbed her phone and called him.

Not because she missed him already. No. It was simply a matter of expediency. She needed to know his plans to see if they meshed with hers. Yes, that was it. She didn't miss his infrequent smile, or the way he looked at her with such heat, or his surprisingly teasing manner.

He kept calling his security specialists *goons* just to rile her up.

She refused to back down on that score though. They'd behaved like goons and she'd let them know it. Strangely enough, both Klaus and Gregor seemed to like and respect her. Gregor had even apologized for pulling a gun on her and promised it wouldn't happen again.

She should hope not. And not to anyone else either. When she'd said so, he'd just given her a slightly enigmatic smile and walked away.

~ ~ ~

Lysander picked up after the first ring.

"Hello, *glikia mou*. Have you changed your mind about coming over tonight?" he asked in a tone meant for the bedroom.

Sudden heat washed over Rowan and she fanned herself with a piece of junk mail. He'd taken to calling her *his sweet* and the endearment did things to her all on its own. In that tone? It was deadly.

"I was wondering if you had plans to attend any events that I've been invited to," she said. "I try to go to at least a couple while my parents are in Athens, and I would prefer to make it an opportunity to see you as well."

Her father's business interests in Greece were a big part of his company's revenue, but her parents still spent the majority of their time in their home outside of Atlanta. Her mother enjoyed her social position there as a Queen Bee around whom many buzzed, more than in Athens where she was not married to one of the wealthiest men in any room.

Oh, her father was rich all right, but he didn't make the Forbes list. Lysander was near the top and Cyrus was nearer the bottom, but he was still on it.

"You could have called my personal assistant for that," he said, his tone teasing. "And yet you called me."

"You've given me access to your PA?" Rowan asked with shock she made no attempt to hide.

Neither her father, nor Cyrus, had done so. They expected full access to her schedule, but had never returned the favor. She'd spent so much of her life in a controlled bubble, she thought disconsolately.

"Yes." Lysander's response was tinged with surprise at his own behavior. "I have just sent details to your phone. Did you want to call her instead?"

"No. I want to talk to you," Rowan offered with more honesty than was prudent.

"And I am pleased to speak with you," he said, rewarding her truthfulness with his own, his tone warm and approving.

"Lysander..." She let her voice trail off, not sure what she wanted to say.

"Have you accomplished the chores you set out to do?" he asked.

She nodded, remembered they weren't facetiming and said, "I've started them anyway."

"Ah, you are going through your mail," he guessed. "One benefit to being a billionaire executive is that I have people to do that for me."

"So, if I sent you a card or a letter, your PA would read it before you did?" she asked, her voice going sultry. "I'd better be careful what I write then."

"Just as any correspondence from my mother has special instructions to be brought directly to me, so does yours."

"It does? Already?" They'd only been seeing each other for a minute.

And really, they hadn't even had their first date. They'd spent the weekend together, mostly in bed.

"I am an efficient man."

"I wish I was as efficient. I have another load of laundry to do and my apartment needs a good dusting and vacuuming." She'd meant to do it on the weekend, but those plans had gone by the wayside in the face of the opportunity to spend that time with him.

"If I offered to send a cleaning service so you could return to my home, would you be charmed, or offended?"

"Good question." But her heart had already answered it. She was definitely charmed.

He wanted to spend time with her and that he was pressing for her return to his home when he made a habit of working long hours and into the night, meant he planned to change his own schedule to make that worth it. Didn't he?

She said, "It depends on if you plan to spend time with me out of bed if I return to the villa, or just want a convenient bed partner."

"If I planned to work while you were here, I would not ask you to come," he said with easy assurance.

He hadn't had to think about his answer for even a second. Which meant what? Lysander really did want to spend time with her.

"This thing between us, it's intense, isn't it?"

"Yes."

"That's kind of scary."

"It doesn't need to be. Neither of us has made any promises."

That wasn't as reassuring as she was sure he thought it would be.

"I don't live with women."

Well, that had come out of nowhere. "I wasn't asking to move in. You're the one trying to finagle my presence in your home, if you'll remember."

"I am aware." He paused like he was thinking. "I don't live with my lovers," he said again. "But I want to live with you. You are right, most nights I work after dinner and I leave early for the office, but I want to spend as much time with you as possible."

She should be shocked, but she wasn't. Because Rowan wanted the same thing. Whatever they had between them, it was burning hot and bright right now. She wanted to indulge in every second that blazing hot passion lasted. It was bound to burn itself out, but until then?

Rowan wanted to spend every available moment with Lysander.

"Not just in bed," she said, certain that she could not live with that kind of arrangement. It would just be another box to stuff herself into and she was done being stifled.

"Not just in bed," he affirmed. "I want to eat breakfast with you, even if it's two hours after I've started my workday. I want to see you when I return to my home, to find you watching your favorite show or haranguing my security men about their manners."

"That sounds very domestic."

"I have never said I don't like domesticity."

Only commitment. "All right."

"You will move in with me?" he asked.

"Well, I had been thinking about getting a cat. I guess that will have to wait."

"You want a cat?"

"Yes." Getting a rescue pet had never been an option when she was living at home or in the Andino mansion. "But it can wait. I'm keeping my apartment though. This thing between us could fizzle out in a week."

"Or not."

"Or not. Either way, I'm keeping my place."

"Naturally."

"And I'm not coming over tonight," she said firmly. Both for his sake and her own. "I'm going to finish my laundry and pack some things like a normal person. I'll come to the villa tomorrow after work."

"I will not be home." He sounded chagrined.

He was home now and she was refusing to come over. In way, that was good. He needed to know from the outset that he couldn't have everything his own way.

"Then you'd better give your goons instructions to let me in," she told him saucily.

"They prefer security specialists."

She laughed. Then his rich chuckle came through the phone and she felt like she'd won something.

"Those instructions have already been given regardless," he said.

"You really are efficient."

"Or it is important."

She wasn't touching that. How could she be important to him already? But then, she was upending her own life to be with him, even if it was temporary. He was definitely already important to her.

~ ~ ~

The next evening when she arrived at Lysander's gate, her backseat and trunk full of clothes and other things she needed for an extended stay, Gregor sent it sliding open as soon as he saw her. He smiled and saluted as she drove past.

She smiled back and waived. She noticed a second security guard she hadn't seen before, standing alertly on the other side of the drive, his attention fixed on the area around the gate and not her car. She didn't wave to him, but she did wonder if he was added security, or if she just hadn't noticed him before.

When she stopped her car in front of the villa, Klaus was standing at the top of the steps. Gregor must have called him. Movement flickered in her peripheral vision and she turned her head to see what it was. Another guard walked the perimeter around the house.

Rowan got out of the car and took a moment to really examine her surroundings. She could see two more guards on patrol in the distance.

"The threat to Lysander has increased?" she asked worriedly.

Klaus shrugged. "Not that I am aware. He ordered additional and tighter security last night when he told us you would be moving in."

"I'm not moving in." She shouldered a bag with a long strap and pulled another wheeled suitcase from the car.

"It certainly looks like you're moving in," Klaus drawled.

"I'm staying a while." And that was all he needed to know. "And I'm keeping my own apartment."

Okay, maybe that too. She was no clinger-on, expecting her rich lover to support her financially.

"Does Mr. Baros know that?" Klaus asked skeptically.

Her reply was firm. "Yes."

"If you say so." Klaus stepped forward and opened the back door on the other side of her car and immediately began pulling stuff out.

Since he grabbed her largest case which was unwieldy and had a wonky wheel, she didn't object. When the wheel showed its temperament, the burly security specialist just picked up the bag and carried it.

"Impressive," Rowan quipped. But she meant it. She'd had to strain to get the bag up into her car. "I've got a box of books in the trunk you're free to manhandle as well."

Chapter Eleven

"Are you flirting with my goons?" Lysander asked from the top of the steps.

Rowan spun toward him, knocking over the case she'd been pulling. "Sander! I thought you were going to be gone."

"I took my conference call here. The wi-fi is just as good."

"Wasn't it supposed to last another hour?" He'd told her that, and then asked if she minded waiting to have dinner until later.

Since Rowan had long since adjusted to the European tendency to eat at 8 pm or later, she'd acquiesced easily.

"It is over," he said.

She couldn't help wondering if he'd cut it short to see her. But that was really egotistical, wasn't it? No matter how much he liked her, a man as driven and focused as Lysander wasn't going to cancel an important meeting so he could spend time with her.

He reached her and kissed her. It was no sweet buss of lips to say hello, but a meeting of their mouths that made no attempt to deny the passion between them. By the time she'd been thoroughly greeted the bag she'd been carrying had fallen to the ground as well.

She stared down at it, unable to parse what she was supposed to do now.

"I think you befuddled her, boss."

"Befuddled?" Rowan mouthed to Lysander.

"Klaus is very proud of his vocabulary."

"I like the word befuddled. I've never seen someone it fit so well either."

That had her frowning, though not really upset. "I am not confused."

The look the security specialist gave her put that into question, but all Klaus did was grab the box of books she'd mentioned and ask his boss, "Where do you want these?"

"What are they?" Lysander asked.

"Books."

Lysander looked at Rowan. "You brought books?"

"I like to read." She'd been teased by both her family and her ex for being too bookish. Like that was a bad thing.

"I read business journals."

"No fiction?" she asked, appalled and trying not to show it.

Fiction was amazing.

"Perhaps you will recommend a book."

Well, that was an unexpected response. "Sure."

"Where would you like your books?"

"Anywhere I can find them easily."

"We can put a bookcase in the lounge." That's what he called his inner sanctum.

"Or the bedroom."

"I doubt you'll get much reading done in there."

Rowan almost laughed, but then she thought about it. Though she'd done most of her reading in bed in the past, she had to admit that even she could think of something she'd rather do in there than immerse herself in her favorite fictional worlds.

"The lounge it is then."

Klaus left without having to be instructed further.

"You don't have to install a bookcase just for me." She could keep her books in the box. It wasn't a permanent home for them after all.

Lysander didn't reply. He simply picked up the two bags she'd dropped and headed into his villa with them. Somehow seeing the billionaire carrying her luggage made this move in with him all the more real. Also, she couldn't imagine the other men in his world doing such a mundane chore.

Rowan grabbed the last box from her small trunk. Most of the space was taken up by the large battery that powered her electric car.

She passed Klaus on her way inside. "I'll put your car in the nearest garage, bay two. Your keys will be on a hook by the door."

"Is that secure?" she asked before thinking better of it.

She was for all intents and purposes now living in a secured compound. No one was getting inside without an invitation and Lysander's guests weren't likely to steal a car that could be bought for what they paid in golfing fees yearly, if not monthly.

"It takes a fingerprint to open the door into the garage."

"Oh, then how will I open it?"

"Yours will be added to the biometric lock system."

"That's pretty high tech, isn't it?"

"Television may make it look easy to bypass biometric locks, but it's not, and this system in particular is one of the most secure."

"Not *the* most secure?" she teased.

"Those can be unwieldy, and with our other measures would be overkill," Lysander answered, stopping next to her.

He took the box from her arms without comment, and she let it go. She'd never been averse to gentlemanly behavior, so long as it was not accompanied by an attitude of male superiority.

She arched her brows at him. "I didn't know you and your cohorts thought any security measure could be overkill."

"We're cohorts now?" Klaus asked. "Not goons?"

Rowan ignored him and kept her gaze pinned on Lysander.

He smiled that gorgeous smile that always made her heart flutter. "We do not need military grade tech to protect automobiles."

"Are you saying you have it elsewhere in the villa?" she asked.

"The panic room is second to none for security and ability to withstand efforts to gain entrance."

"Oh." She wondered if he was going to show it to her. She knew that the location of the panic room in her old home was secret to anyone outside the family.

Even the staff who had worked for the Andino the longest had not been told where it was. Rowan had always determined that if there was ever an occasion to use it, she would make sure to bring as many of the staff with her as she could.

Luckily, she'd never had to use it for any reason.

"All the staff and security team know it's location and the domestic staff knows to head there if the need arises."

Rowan cast a glance at Klaus's retreating figure. "And the security staff?"

"If the panic room becomes necessary, it would be because they had been neutralized already."

By neutralized he meant killed. Rowan shuddered. "Being a billionaire isn't without its drawbacks."

Her family home had not had a panic room as her father had never considered one necessary. That Lysander did only showed how aware of his own vulnerability to attack he was. She hated knowing his wealth and position of influence made him a target.

"If you do not want the world to know we are together, we can skip the gala," he said, clearly misinterpreting her look.

"It's not me I'm worried about. It's you. I noticed the increased security."

"It became necessary when you agreed to live here."

"But I'm nobody." Maybe not poor, but certainly not rich in comparison to this man.

"You are my girlfriend. That makes you vulnerable to kidnapping for ransom."

"That only happens in movies," she quipped, knowing it wasn't true. "Besides you aren't going to pay a million dollars to get me back."

"I would pay whatever was necessary, but it is a moot point as you will not be taken."

"What are you going to do, send Klaus with me to work?" she asked facetiously, not as convinced as he was that simply by dating him she became a potential target for kidnappers. "Your mother would be way more at risk than me."

"She has her own security team."

"I'm glad." Rowan liked Iona Baros and didn't want her hurt in some misguided attempt to extort money out of her son.

"It is good to hear you say that. I thought you might balk at having one assigned to you."

"What? That's not necessary."

"For as long as you remain living here, it is."

"But you never said anything about that last night."

He shrugged, like it should have been obvious.

"Are you telling me that you assign security to all your lovers?"

"No."

"What makes me special?" she demanded.

He turned and headed toward the stairs. "What's in this box? Does it go in the bedroom?"

"Probably." It had come out of her bedroom, but she'd stored things wherever they fit in her small apartment. "Now, answer my question. What makes me special?"

They reached his bedroom suite and he placed the box on the table by the settee in the sitting area. "Staff will unpack your cases. Would you like to go for a swim?"

"Yes." Rowan loved the water and had really missed access to a pool since moving into her apartment with no amenities. "But my bathing suit is in one of the cases."

She tried to remember which one she'd packed her swimsuits in. Rowan had pared down to two suits, when she used to have seven. The rest of her clothes had gone through a similar winnowing. There simply wasn't room in her apartment to store a wardrobe meant for a socialite, only a social worker.

"There are a couple for you to choose from in the drawer already."

"You got me swimsuits?" she asked. "You know I thought you were only buying an outfit for me so I could be comfortable and would spend the night."

"I do not buy clothes to get women into bed with me." He headed into the bedroom and then to the walk-in closet that had conspicuously empty racks.

For her clothes. He was quite literally making space for her in his life.

Touched, Rowan started pulling open drawers, only to find most of them already had an item or two of clothing, all clearly meant for her. Even socks and underwear.

She pulled a pair of lace panties out and dangled them on her finger. "There's almost nothing to these." They were just a triangle of lace and three strings. "I can't believe you had a shopper buy these for me."

"I ordered them."

At her askance look, he shrugged. "I had time between meetings and did not want to get immersed in a report."

"So, you went online and bought me underwear."

Color burnished his cheekbones, but he nodded resolutely.

"You're kind of amazing, you know that?" She hugged him tightly. "Thank you."

His arms came around her automatically and he held her close. "You are thanking me for buying you sexy lingerie?"

"One should always express appreciation for a gift," she said in a lecturing tone and then smiled. "I like that you were thinking of me. And I like even more that you personally picked these out. Though I can't promise I'll ever wear them. I know some women just love thongs, but I've always found them uncomfortable."

"I promise that if you put them on you won't wear them long enough to be bothered."

She laughed and stepped away from him. "You promised me a swim."

He indicated a drawer she hadn't opened. "You'll find swimsuits in there."

She opened the drawer and found three suits inside. None of them one-pieces. She did find a tankini, but feeling daring, she opted for a black and white polka dot bikini that reminded her of a 1940s pin up girl. The top supported her ample breasts and the bottom was high waisted, flattering her curves, but not hiding them. A one-piece in a similar style had made it into her keep pile when she'd gone through her clothes.

"This is really me," she said, a little surprised he knew her so well.

It wasn't as if they'd ever been swimming together.

"Your favorite designer has a lot of 1940s inspired styles in her collection," Lysander said with a verbal shrug.

"Well, I love it," Rowan said happily.

Lysander's smile was wolfish. "I'm going to love seeing it on you."

Somehow, they both got their suits on without falling into bed naked together. It was touch and go, but Rowan wanted that swim. She also wanted to know they could spend time together outside the bedroom. That was, after all, a condition of her moving in with him.

She wasn't just a convenient booty call.

And neither was he.

Chapter Twelve

Lysander dived gracefully into the pool and immediately started swimming laps.

Rowan opted for entry into the water via the steps, but she dove under as soon as she reached water deep enough to swim in and began her own laps, swimming in the opposite direction to him, so they passed each other on every lap. She didn't know how long they'd been doing laps when she felt that perfect release from tension that swimming gave her.

Soon after, she finished her laps and stopped in the shallow end of the pool. Lysander executed a quick turn at the wall in the deep end and then joined her seconds later, erupting out of the water like Poseidon.

Gorgeous and powerful.

And his gaze was locked on her.

Needing to focus on anything but his nearly naked body, she brought up the security detail again. "You never explained why I have to have bodyguards when the other women you've dated didn't."

"I have never invited a woman to live with me." He brushed his hand over his wet hair, causing rivulets to travel enticingly down his neck and over his shoulders. "I don't even bring my lovers back to my home."

She wanted to follow those drops of water with her fingertips...maybe her tongue.

Forcing her attention back on the discussion, she asked "Where do you take them?" She couldn't imagine a man with his need for control being okay with all the sex happening at his lover's home.

"That is what hotel suites are for."

"Huh." She waived her arms back and forth through the water, loving its silky feeling against her skin. "Not the point right now, but just so you know, I'm not adverse to hotel rooms. They're a little impersonal to be the exclusive venue for such an intimate relationship though."

"Sex is not always intimate." He sounded very definite.

She was just as definite. "It is with us, though."

"Yes."

She smiled. "Still not sure I get why me temporarily moving into your villa makes me a target for extortionists."

"You are clearly important to me, different from my other lovers."

"Are all billionaires as paranoid as you?" she wondered out loud.

"They should be, but some show more concern for the security of their cars than the safety of the people in their inner circle."

Thinking of some of the billionaires that made it into the media, especially back in the States, Rowan had to agree. "I don't think I want a security detail."

"They can accompany you, or follow you. Your choice."

In other words, she was getting security if she wanted it or not. How easy it would be for her guards to protect her would be determined by her actions.

She sighed. "You're not going to budge on this, are you?"

"No."

"Okay, but fair warning, I'm putting them to work when they come with me to the org." There was always stuff that needed doing and never enough staff or volunteers to do it.

"So long as they are in the same room with you, or the room through which anyone would have to go to get to you, that is fine."

Not sure the security specialists would agree with him while stuffing the job placement packs with reading material and the donations from companies wanting the people her org served to feel valued and seen. Regardless, Rowan couldn't help but smile at the thought of another set of helping hands.

"You are pleased to have the help?"

"Yes."

"If not the protection."

"That's nice too, in a way." It made her feel like he cared about her, or at least her safety. But she added with honesty, "It might get a little stifling as well."

"We make sacrifices for the life we choose to live."

"True." She made a faster move with her arm than those before and a wave of water arced up and splashed him. "You have sacrificed your almost dry face."

He laughed and sent water cascading over her. Her hair was already wet, so she just laughed. They splashed and played until they ended up plastered against each other in water too deep for her to stand.

She wrapped her legs around his waist and her arms around his neck. "I like this."

"I do too." His eyes were dark with unmistakable passion.

She'd been playing, but he was thinking about a whole other kind of physical exercise than swimming.

It sparked a response in Rowan that whooshed through her like a tsunami of sensual need. "Do you think they'll hold dinner?"

"Yes," he growled before kissing her breathless.

Water was covering her lower face before Rowan realized what was happening. Lysander wasn't paying attention to where they were, and he had been shifting toward the deeper end.

She broke the kiss, inhaled some water, coughed and started laughing. "I thought making love in the pool was supposed to be sexy."

Lysander was already moving them the opposite direction with quick strides in the water and soon only her feet dangled in it.

"It is," he assured her, before sitting on a tiled cement bench that went down both sides of the shallow end of the pool. He pulled her astride his lap. "It is," he said again, his mouth taking hers before she could reply.

Rowan lost all thought of saying anything as passion once again erupted inside her. Oh sheesh, she hoped his staff were nowhere around because she had the feeling things were about to get very sexy indeed.

"Do not worry," he said as he unhooked her bikini top and caressed her back. "I gave instructions for privacy."

"What about the patrolling guards?" she asked, stopping him removing her top entirely by pressing her arms down to hold the fabric in place.

"No patrols on this side until I give the word."

"That's safe?"

"We have motion sensors on the wall and cameras covering every angle but the pool itself right now. That camera will be turned back on at my instruction."

"You planned for this."

"Rowan, you are irresistible to me. I always plan for the possibility of this." He canted his hips upward, letting her feel the hardness of his erection.

With her legs splayed over him, his hardon pressed against her clitoris and she moaned, pushing downward with her hips to increase the friction. The two swimsuits stopped anything but contact that teased at pleasure.

She climbed off his lap, her gaze locked on his. "No one can see us?"

"No."

"You promise?"

"You have my word."

She pulled her top away from her body and tossed it to the side of the pool, her nipples going instantly hard in the evening air. It felt so good, she moaned a little and then she reached down to remove her bottoms. It was easier than she expected. Unlike a wet swimsuit outside the pool, the fabric glided down her legs, helped by the water.

Throwing it in a pile with her top, she motioned with her other hand toward Lysander. "Now you."

With a choked sound, her lover surged to his feet and shoved his suit off too, not bothering to retrieve it from the water before pulling her against him and kissing her with open mouthed passion.

The water ebbed and flowed around them adding to the sensations bombarding Rowan. Seconds later, he'd maneuvered them back to the bench and she was once again astride his lap, but no fabric separated her sex from his. This time when they arched together, his erection pressed directly against her pleasure spot, rubbing up and down as they shifted together in the water.

She rode him like he was inside her, the water acting as a lubricant that allowed smooth movement. The stimulation to her clitoris felt amazing.

"That feels so damn good, *glikia mou*."

"Yes, it does." Was that throaty purr her?

Lysander brought out a sexual side that Rowan hadn't known existed in her and she reveled in every ecstatic second.

He cupped her breasts, squeezing and brushing his thumbs over her nipples. Rowan increased the speed of her thrusts. So did Lysander so they were rutting together in a beautiful frenzy.

The water added to the pleasure, but it also made it hard for her to get enough sensation to tip over. It all felt too wonderful to stop though.

One of Lysander's hands slid down her back, over her bottom and between her thighs. He pressed a single finger inside her, and Rowan's vaginal walls contracted around it. Now every thrust brought pleasure to her most sensitive flesh both inside and out.

Pleasure coiled tightly in her belly and then exploded, fireworks going off in her body as ecstasy roared over her. Lysander thrust upward sending aftershocks of pleasure through her as his body went rigid and he shouted with release.

Rowan collapsed against him, her head resting on his shoulder. Her lungs were working like bellows, but then so were his.

"Definitely sexy," she managed between gasping breaths.

"Yes, you are."

It was a cheesy line, but the sincerity in his tone and the way he held her close made it something more. Lysander didn't need Rowan to be thinner, or less chatty, or anything different than exactly what she was, to be sexually enthralled with her.

She would take it.

If her heart insisted there should be more, she ignored that little voice in favor of the sense of repletion she felt.

"I'm so glad you arranged for our privacy. This was amazing."

"Even if we had not made love, I would not have wanted the staff watching our every move. Sometimes, it is good simply not to have eyes of other people on you."

"Even security?" she asked.

"When our safety can be assured, yes."

Oh, she noticed that caveat. He wasn't backing down about her having a bodyguard. Rowan let it go.

She'd lived with some level of security most of her life, though it had increased after marriage. She'd only known full autonomy since leaving Cyrus.

And if having a bodyguard was the price she had to pay for being Lysander's lover, she would pay it happily.

Chapter Thirteen

The morning of the Vasileiou Gala dawned bright and sunny, as most did this time of year in Athens.

Rowan watched the sunrise from her spot on the terrace, a cup of coffee in front of her. Lysander had risen at 4:30 for an international video conference. Rowan usually went back to sleep after he left the bed, but not this morning.

She was going to see her parents and her ex-husband, as well as his family. Tension thrummed through her at the prospect.

Her mother had called to confirm that Rowan would be at the gala. Confirming her intention to attend, Rowan hadn't mentioned who her date would be. Nor had Rowan told her mother that she wouldn't be sitting with them.

"What has you up so early?" Lysander's deep voice had Rowan turning from the sunrise to face him.

He was dressed immaculately in one of his bespoke suits, a crisp white shirt and perfectly knotted tie. She was sure her lover had made an impressive sight on the video call, as he always did.

Anyone interacting with Lysander Baros knew the man was put together and powerful. But she, little ole' Rowan Johnson, had seen him disheveled and naked.

It gave Rowan an intrinsic thrill to be one of the few people in the world to know more than just the public persona. She had witnessed the real man: the loving son, the passionate and surprisingly earthy lover, the charming friend.

She had a bookcase in his inner sanctum and closet space in his bedroom suite.

"I couldn't go back to sleep after you left. I thought I would watch the sunrise."

Lysander put his hand on her shoulder, his thumb brushing along her neck. "One of the things I enjoy most about this property is the ability to watch either the sunrise or sunset in comfort from a terrace, or a balcony."

"I do too."

"But the sunrise is not what got you out of bed this morning."

She sighed and shook her head. "No, it isn't."

"Are you stressed about seeing Cyrus tonight?" Lysander asked, his tone carefully neutral.

"Not as tense as I am about seeing my parents," Rowan admitted.

Lysander moved to take the chair on the other side of the small table. His dark gaze bore into hers. "Why?"

"Unlike your mother, mine constantly looks for fault and isn't shy about voicing her criticism."Rowan grimaced. "Unless she helped pick it out, my dress is never right for the occasion. Same with the amount of makeup I choose to wear, and she's appalled I won't get a weekly manicure like she does."

"Does it help to know that I think you look lovely?" he asked, waggling his sexy eyebrows.

She laughed. "How do you know? You haven't seen what I picked out for tonight."

"It won't matter. You are beautiful, with or without makeup. So long as your clothing isn't some monstrosity intended to hide your figure, it will be gorgeous because it will be on you."

Warmth spread through Rowan. "That's a very nice thing to say."

"I am not a nice man."

He did have a reputation for ruthlessness in business, but since that ruthless attitude rarely got directed toward the rank-and-file employees, she didn't hold it against him.

Personally, Rowan thought that the management Lysander was known for winnowing were probably not *all that*. Or her lover would never let them go. He was too savvy for blunders like that.

"Maybe to other people, but you are to me."

"It is not kindness when it is truth," he said in a tone that sounded like a warning.

She merely shook her head in response. He wanted her to think he would be ruthless with her, and they both knew he would not. Not until it came time to say goodbye. For however long this thing between them lasted, Rowan had a unique position in Lysander's life, similar to his mother's.

"I guarantee my mother won't agree and my father will be livid I'm not sitting with him and trying to make things up with Cyrus."

"It is unfortunate that he will be angry, but that was the point of this, wasn't it?" Lysander reached across the table and took her hand.

He was always touching her. A fingertip brushing along her jawline. Sitting close enough to her on the couch so their thighs touched, and he could easily put his arm over her shoulders. But her favorite was how he cupped her nape.

That gave her shivers every time. And it made her feel special. There was not a single photo of Lysander in the tabloids or society pages touching a woman in a similar way. Yes, Rowan had paid attention over the years. She'd been curious.

Her inner voice said now might be the time to admit it had been more than innocent curiosity, but Rowan wasn't admitting anything. Not even to herself.

When she didn't reply, Lysander asked, "You wanted to let both families know that you are unequivocally over Cyrus and have moved on from your failed marriage, did you not?"

"Yes." She sighed. "In theory anyway." In practice, facing the guaranteed censure from her family made acid churn in Rowan's stomach.

He tugged at her hand until she was standing and then pulled her to him and into his lap. "If you want to cancel tonight, we can." He kissed the corner of her lips. "My donation is the same whether I attend, or not."

Rowan sucked in a shocked breath at the offer. She knew attending this gala was important to Lysander, though she did not know why. He never missed.

"No." She turned her head so his dark brown eyes could see the sincerity in hers. "Thank you for offering that. It means a lot, but no. We are going. I will deal with my parents like I have always done."

The best she could and with antacids tucked into her evening bag.

"This time I will be with you."

It was a sweet sentiment, if not as reassuring as she was sure he intended it to be. What could Lysander do to mitigate motherly disapproval, or fatherly disappointment?

~ ~ ~

The answer to that question came later in the evening.

Rowan walked into the gala, her hand tucked in the crook of Lysander's tuxedo clad arm and chatter had started immediately.

She heard things like, "Isn't that Rowan Andino with Lysander Baros?" and "What is she doing here? I thought she'd moved back to the States."

Lysander ignored it all and Rowan did her best to pretend she did too, though the back of her neck was hot with embarrassment. She kept her head up though and her face placid as she and Lysander followed the server leading them to their table.

Her father stepped in front of them, his expression stern, forcing the server to halt.

Lysander had no choice but to stop as well, though he did it so naturally, it seemed like stopping to talk to her father was Lysander's idea.

"Mr. Johnson." Lysander acknowledged her father with a slight dip of his chin.

"Mr. Baros, my daughter's seat is over there." He pointed to the table where her mother sat with the Andinos.

"You are mistaken." Though his face showed not the slightest emotion, Lysander's voice was cold as the arctic. "She is sitting with me."

"But Cyrus bought her ticket."

"My brother may have purchased an extra ticket, but it was not for *my* companion."

Her father turned away from Lysander's steady, unperturbed gaze, turning his look of disapproval on her. "You knew we were expecting you at our table," he hissed in an undertone.

"If you will excuse us," Lysander said to her father as if he hadn't spoken and subtly shifted his body forward.

Now, if he didn't want to create a scene, her father was the one who had no choice but to move.

"Rowan," he barked as she followed Lysander.

"Do not acknowledge him," Lysander instructed, his voice loud enough to carry, his arm dropping around her waist. "If he cannot speak to you in a polite tone, he won't be speaking to you at all."

Rowan couldn't remember the last time someone had taken umbrage on her behalf like that, much less publicly stood up for her.

Lysander did not allow the server to pull out Rowan's chair, insisting on doing it himself. Once she was seated, he introduced her to the others at their table.

"My mother, you know," he said. "This is her companion, Garret Landry."

"That sounds like an English name," Rowan said after the usual *pleasure to meet you*.

"American," Mr. Landry said with a smile that he turned on Iona. "Apparently like mother like son."

Iona's pleased expression showed how much she enjoyed the man saying that about her and Lysander. Rowan liked the comparison too. It implied that she and Lysander were a real couple.

Which they were, even if their time together had an as yet unspecified sell-by date.

Lysander continued his introductions his attitude that of a man both pleased by and proud of his companion.

Rowan learned that the rest of the table was made up of high-level managers in his company. Inviting them to share his table had been a nice thing to do.

Buying the table cost six figures. She knew because the Andinos bought one each year. However, her father-in-law used his tickets to curry favor with other tycoons and their wives. Her own father had to reimburse Baptiste for his and her mother's tickets, if he wanted to sit at the table with them.

Lysander could have used the gala as an opportunity to gain kudos with business associates too, but he opted to give his management team the chance to make connections at the prestigious event.

Which showed just how confident he was that they wouldn't leave his employment.

Time passed much faster than it usually did at events like this for Rowan. She liked Lysander's people and they liked the positive influence she had on him. More than one had remarked on how much more relaxed Lysander was with her there. One even said he'd been in a better mood since she'd moved into his villa.

"You knew I moved in?" she asked the man, and then turned to address Lysander. "You told them?"

"No." He frowned at his manager. "I am the same as I've always been."

"If you say so, boss," said one of the women at the table and then she smiled at Rowan. "The paparazzi have nothing on the office grapevine."

"They must not because news of my move hasn't made it into the papers yet." Rowan was fully expecting a distressed phone call from her mother when it did and a lecture from her father when he found out.

"After tonight, you can bet they'll be watching at the gate with their telephoto lenses and microphones, hoping to get a comment," the same woman said.

Rowan wasn't worried. She'd dealt with her share of the gossip press while married to Cyrus and more than when news of the divorce became public.

To avoid them, she'd spent a few months in the United States after filing for divorce in a state court. However, she had a job to do and a life to build as Rowan Johnson, not Andino, in Greece.

She'd returned to Athens months before the divorce was finalized and for a while the gutter media hounded her every step.

Lysander's security was pretty tight right now because of the threats made against him. The press would find her a lot harder to access than she had been after she moved into her apartment.

"Rowan will have security to run interference for her," Lysander said.

Was that one of the reasons he'd insisted on her having bodyguards?

"Good," the woman said.

"I'm glad," Iona added with a look of approval for her son. "She deserves looking after."

"I can look after myself," Rowan felt compelled to point out, but once again she felt something warm inside her at the knowledge Lysander was watching out for her.

"But you needn't. The paparazzi can be so tiresome," Iona added. "I dealt with them for years because there was no secret who my son's father was."

Rowan hadn't considered that aspect of Baptiste Andino acknowledging his illegitimate son.

"The security detail my son has assigned to me make sure I am not bothered by reporters now. Their photos..." Iona waived her hand in dismissal.

"You cannot hide from the cameras, but I do not care if they take my picture. Only if they don't get my good side."

Everyone at the table laughed. Including Rowan. "I know what you mean. They're very good at taking pictures that get you at your worst so they can run stories with all sorts of speculation. One tabloid insinuated that Cyrus and I had divorced because I had a drug problem. The pictures they ran with the article made it look like it could be true."

"Disgusting," Mr. Landry said. "I hope you sued them for libel."

"I didn't need to. They ran a retraction before the other outlets had picked up the story. I guess Cyrus didn't want even his ex-wife besmirching his reputation that way."

"That wasn't Mr. Andino," an affable man who had been introduced as Lysander's media liaison, said. "That was all Lysander. He instructed me to get the story quashed and I did."

Chapter Fourteen

Rowan was flummoxed. Lysander had forced the retraction? But why?

She turned to him, needing to know. Why was this ruthless billionaire her secret knight in shining armor? "Why would you do that?"

"You were dealing with enough and I don't like the gutter press."

She had no doubt that was true, but it didn't explain why he'd wielded his immense power on her behalf. There were dozens of licentious and libelous stories out there he could have turned his attention to.

But he'd protected *her*.

"He gave me permission to set the big dogs on them." The media liaison named a prestigious and exclusive law firm.

The look Lysander gave him, said the media liaison had been a little too open about his activities on her behalf. The younger man stopped talking and took a hasty sip of his water.

Rowan felt badly for him, but she was glad to know Lysander deserved the White Knight credit and not her ex. Even if she still didn't understand why.

"Wow. Well thank you. It helped. A lot." She'd handled everything else to that point with a pretty even keel, but being accused of drug addiction with those awful pictures as proof had hurt. "If that story had gained traction, my boss would have had no choice but to fire me. The organization can't afford to be associated with that kind of story."

Her director had brought her into his office and told her that very thing. Rowan had been devastated, but then the tabloid had printed the retraction, on the front page no less. Her life had been allowed to go on as normal and she'd kept her job.

She didn't know why Lysander had protected her. They hadn't even been friends then. But she was grateful for it.

He had all the makings of a fairytale knight, but she needed to remember that this story didn't have a happily ever after. No matter what her heart kept insisting it wanted.

She needed to be content with happy for right now. Because she was.

Very happy.

"That is my son, a gentleman and a protector," Iona said complacently. "He is too soft hearted for his own good sometimes, but in this case, I can only applaud his instinct to protect."

The people around the table reacted to that statement with varying degrees of amusement and disbelief.

Lysander shook his head, his own expression well...cranky. "You see me through the eyes of a mother's love. I assure you, I am not soft."

Rowan could attest to that. As soon as she had the thought, she nearly choked on her before-dinner champagne. *Naughty Rowan*, she chastised herself, but the urge to laugh at her own private little joke was still there.

"Are you alright?" Lysander demanded.

"I'm..." She sucked in air for several seconds. "Fine. Just swallowed my champagne wrong."

"Perhaps wine without bubbles?" he asked, looking at the expensive champagne like it was pig swill.

"It wasn't the champagne. It was something I thought...it was funny and I started to laugh, but I was drinking." She shrugged. "Not a great combination."

Lysander's expression turned thoughtful, and she knew he was replaying their recent conversation in his head. She could see the moment he realized what had amused her.

He leaned forward and said sotto voce, "I am never *soft* when I am around you."

Rowan laughed again, the sound low and throaty, garnering several speculative looks from the others at their table.

But no one said anything, and the conversation turned to the Greece National Lacrosse Team and its chances of making a showing in international competition.

Rowan knew the team had been created in 2018 and that was about it. She wasn't big on sports, much preferring a comfy chair and a good book for her downtime. Several guests were clear enthusiasts though and the conversation carried them through the starter and into the main course.

Lysander was knowledgeable, but not keenly interested, though no one else at the table seemed to notice that.

Huh.

"Does your company support a lacrosse team?" Rowan asked him as she cut into what looked like a perfectly cooked sea bream filet. It flaked apart with her fork, no knife required.

"Several of my subsidiary holdings field teams for competition. It has become a near mania." He gave her a look. "Few things can make me that excited."

That look said she was one of them.

Heat washed through her, and Rowan smiled. "I can return the compliment."

"I didn't say anything."

"Didn't you?"

His smile was all the answer she needed.

"I have never seen the boss smile this much in a year," the media liaison said, back to his chatty self. "Not even when we managed to quash all rumors of a takeover so the stock didn't rise before he could make his move."

"He was talking about the many lacrosse teams the subsidiary companies in Baros International field."

"I'm on one. It's a lot of fun," said another man at the table. "But Baros International is a sponsor for the national team."

"I hadn't realized that."

"We have a budget for that sort of thing and one of my management team was passionate about it, so..." Lysander shrugged, like donating millions to supporting a new national sport was no big deal.

"It's not really your thing though, is it?" Rowan asked, wanting to know if she'd read him right.

He shook his head. "No, I am a traditional man and football is my sport of choice."

Rowan remembered learning how popular what they called soccer back home was in Europe. Some businesses even shut down so employees could watch the world cup.

"You may prefer football, but I don't think you're much of a traditionalist."

"You do not?" he asked, his brows raised.

What did that mean? "Considering our current situation, no."

"Oh ho, she has your number my son," Iona said with glee. "My son who sees himself as *traditional*, does he marry? No. Does he give me grandbabies to dote on? He does not!"

Rowan was in danger of choking on her champagne again, so she set the glass down and reached for her water. But Iona cracked her up. The mom who had lived anything but a conventional life, wanted her son to settle down and get married.

And give her grandchildren.

The sincerity of the desire was there in her eyes, though it was not accompanied by the censure her words might have indicated.

So, although Iona did not see her son as perfect, that did not bother her. Not like Rowan's parents.

Speaking of Rowan's parents. What were they doing coming toward Lysander's table when the main course hadn't even been cleared?

It wasn't at all appropriate and could easily cause the kind of scene they both abhorred.

"Rowan, dear, I think there must be some misunderstanding. You were meant to sit at our table." Her mother's opening salvo was only surprising in its timing, not its content.

"I received no invitation," Rowan said calmly. "And as you can see, I am here with Lysander."

Her mother's mouth pursed like she'd just bitten into a lemon, her expression as sour as the fruit too. "I cannot imagine why, but it would be better if you joined us. You sitting here is causing all sorts of speculation."

"Is it?" Rowan asked. "If people are guessing that Lysander and I are a couple, they are right."

"Nonsense. You are married to Cyrus," her father said in a crushing undertone.

Rowan wasn't crushed. In fact, unlike most times when her parents joined forces to castigate her, she didn't feel small at all. She was proud to be here with Lysander and positively wallowed in the joy of being his lover.

"I am not married to Cyrus. Our divorce finalized over a month ago. I have not lived with him in over a year."

"Mr. and Mrs. Johnson, it would be best if you returned to your seats. You are causing far more gossip than your daughter is by being with me."

"Like hell we are. Everyone is talking about it," her father said more loudly than he probably meant to.

"Good," Rowan said firmly. "My marriage to Cyrus is over and the sooner you all come to terms with that, the better."

"Are you *trying* to humiliate the man you said vows to?" her mother asked with freezing censure.

"He negated those vows very early in our marriage if I had but known it. Again, *we are divorced*," Rowan emphasized.

"And furthermore..." she let her own voice rise just enough that the tables around could hear her if they were listening, as she could tell many were.

Her parents really hadn't thought this through.

"There is nothing humiliating to Cyrus in his ex-wife dating his brother. He's lucky to be related to a man as amazing as Lysander and I'm sure he knows it." Even if her ex was too proud to ever admit it out loud. "The key word there is *ex* and who I date has absolutely nothing to do with Cyrus, or you two for that matter. No more than who I choose to live with."

"Live with?" her mother practically shrieked.

Ooops. She hadn't meant to let that particular cat out of the bag at tonight's gala.

That's what came from waiting so long to stand up to her parents. Her primary way of dealing with them since becoming an adult had been to avoid them as much as possible and not do anything to draw their attention and inevitable criticism.

That strategy had been blown out of the water when she filed for divorce, but even then, she'd never come right out and said that they had no say in her life.

"Yes, live with," Lysander said, twining his fingers through Rowan's and then setting their joined hands on the table in full display.

After letting his action sink in for a count of two, he looked off to his left and nodded. Seconds later, servers appeared to usher her parents back to their table. Klaus also stood a couple of feet away, clearly ready to step in if necessary.

Rowan felt badly for the embarrassment both her parents had to be feeling in that moment, but she also acknowledged that they'd brought it on themselves. Trying to spirit her away from Lysander's table in the middle of dinner? Ridiculous.

And not something she would ever have guessed they would do. She'd expected a frontal assault like this, but after dessert when many guests would get up and move around.

"You moved in with my son?" Iona asked, her lovely eyes the same warm brown as Lysander's wide with shock. "I did not realize you two had been dating that long."

"She has a bookcase in my inner sanctum," Lysander said by way of an answer, sidestepping the length of their dating relationship entirely.

If possible, Iona's eyes grew wider. "You installed furniture for her?"

"It's just a bookcase. I think Lysander was offended by the look of my carboard box of books on the floor of his room."

"Certainly, I had no desire to trip over it, but so long as you live there, my house is your home and should accommodate you accordingly."

Iona sucked in a shocked breath of air, but she wasn't the only one. Every person at the table looked gobsmacked at the idea of Lysander making that sort of claim.

A little dumbfounded herself, she was not at all offended.

After dinner, Lysander asked Rowan to dance. Remembering that dance they had shared years ago, she agreed without hesitation.

Their bodies fit together smoothly, and it was as if they had been dancing together for all the years in between.

Lysander held her close, his body heat reaching out to her, his muscular thighs rubbing against her own during certain moments. Forgetting the crowd surrounding them, Rowan gave herself up to the pleasure of being in his arms and moving to the music.

Someone tapped on Lysander's shoulder, and he tensed. Rowan looked up and into her ex-husband's mocking eyes. He thought he had them over a barrel, but only because he didn't understand his half-brother's character.

"Get lost," Lysander said without compunction.

Just as she'd expected him to.

And then he danced her away from Cyrus, who stood fuming and who had finally, truly been humiliated. But only because he'd tried to get Rowan to dance with him, believing that social conventions would force her to comply.

"You do not mind?" Lysander asked as they once again found the rhythm of the music with their bodies.

"No. If you hadn't said it, I would have." The very idea of Cyrus touching her, even for nothing more than a dance, made Rowan's skin crawl.

"He is an idiot."

"When you're right, you're right."

They danced through another song without interruption, heat building between them as it always did when their bodies were so close.

Until another unwelcome voice shattered the intimate bubble around them. This time the voice was feminine.

Chapter Fifteen

"Mon ami, Lysander, what a pleasant surprise," the voice coming from behind Rowan could be no other than Adele Fournier.

Of course, she was at the gala, Rowan thought with a dose of sarcasm she tried to keep off her face.

Lysander stopped dancing, but he kept his arms around Rowan.

Adele laid her hand on Lysander's arm. "Shall we?"

The tall, willowy blond was sophisticated with an ethereal beauty often remarked upon by the press. Tonight, she was dressed to impress in a form fitting copper colored silk gown cut low in the front, making it impossible for her to be wearing one of the designer bras she modeled.

Rowan looked up at Lysander, wondering what he would do.

He was looking back, his expression asking her how *she* planned to respond. He had sent Cyrus on his way. Now, it was her turn.

Rowan gave Adele her best plastic social smile. "I'm afraid Lysander's dance card is full."

The supermodel looked her up and down and then focused on Lysander. "Is she why you aren't answering my texts or calls? Couldn't bypass the opportunity to stick it to your brother by bedding his wife?"

Lysander's big body stiffened and the air around them supercharged. Too busy trying to gauge Rowan's reaction to her barb to notice, Adele remained oblivious. Rowan knew why Lysander was with her and it wasn't to stick it to Cyrus.

They were so hot together, the sheets should be ash after every time they touched.

"Rowan is living in my house because I want her there. Because I want *her.*"

Adele's gaze snapped back to Lysander, her expression one of disbelief.

Rowan's billionaire wasn't done though. "If I had wanted to be that petty in regard to my brother, it was taken care of the first time I had sex with you, wasn't it?"

Without waiting for Adele's reaction, Lysander swept Rowan back into movement and away from the frowning supermodel.

"What did you mean? Was Adele one of Cyrus's women?"

"They had an affair a few years ago. She broke it off with him when she learned about Delphine."

So, him being married hadn't bothered the other woman, but that he already had a mistress did? Typical. "And then she came after you?"

"Yes. Once I learned she had been in his bed, I told her she had to stay away from him if she wanted our arrangement to continue."

"It didn't bother you that she'd been with Cyrus first?"

"I didn't care what men she took to her bed, or how many. Ours was a transactional relationship. She got entrée into events like this and I got a companion that didn't expect anything beyond it."

That made Adele sound more like an escort than a girlfriend. Nothing against escorts, but if he had hired someone to attend functions with him, word would have gotten out and the press would have had a field day.

Just like they were bound to do with her moving into his house. His half-brother's ex-wife.

"Wow. I thought my sex-with-you-to-get-rid-of-Cyrus plot was such an outlandish idea and now I find out I'm the second one to think of it."

"Adele wanted revenge. Full stop. You wanted to give your ex a message that could not be misinterpreted."

Whatever their motives, clearly both she and the supermodel had desired Lysander. Still did from what Rowan could see. Adele had been willing to stay away from Cyrus to keep her no-strings access to his half-brother.

Whereas, Rowan had moved into his home against her own better judgment. But Lysander had made a commitment to her, even if it was temporary.

And he hadn't hesitated to reject Adele's overtures now.

Lysander pulled her just a little bit closer to his hard body, like he couldn't help himself. "I looked into your prenup."

That was not what she expected him to say, so it took Rowan a moment to respond. "Oh?"

She'd given him a copy the day after she moved into his house, but he hadn't brought it up again. She'd assumed Lysander hadn't had time to read it. He was a busy man, working long hours to increase his billions, after all.

"Find anything interesting?"

"I put my team onto researching property purchases and tax shelters created in your name during your marriage. Not only did you get ten percent of Cyrus's company in the divorce, but you retained ownership of a plot of land that wasn't worth much when he bought it."

"You mean he intended it to be a loss to write off?" she asked.

"Precisely."

"But?" She knew there was a *but* or Lysander would not have brought it up.

"He has gone into business with a development company. They need ownership of that parcel of land for the development to go ahead."

"Why?" she wondered out loud.

"There are utility accesses they cannot get with the land they purchased that is adjacent to it."

"Wouldn't it be cheaper to bribe officials?" She knew Cyrus had done exactly that in the past.

"It is not merely a matter of permits, but accessibility."

"What do you mean?"

"There is no connection point to the main utilities if they do not have access to your parcel to lay the connecting lines and pipes."

"Okay, then why not buy it from me? He had to realize I'd have no idea of its value and be willing to sell."

"As to that, I think we covered it with my first statement."

Cyrus was so caught up in his own machinations, it hadn't occurred to him to simply try to buy the land from her.

"With the development in the offing, that piece of land is worth millions."

"If it will get him to leave me alone once and for all, I'll give it to him and good riddance." Marveling, she looked up into Lysander's handsome features. "I can't believe you figured this all out so quickly."

She was sure Cyrus had done his best to cover his tracks and his motives. Rowan would never have thought to even look into the assets she'd gained in the divorce, happy to leave that to her lawyer and accountant.

"My people are good."

She loved that Lysander didn't feel the need to take all the credit.

"Well, they have an amazingly astute boss."

His smile flashed and then he kissed her. Right there in the middle of the dance floor. And she loved it.

Uncaring of what others at the charity gala thought, Rowan kissed him back.

"You aren't giving that land to my half-brother."

Looking deliciously befuddled from the kiss that left him hard as a rock, it took Rowan a beat to focus and parse Lysander's words.

He waited.

Her brows drew together in a frown. "Why not? Is there something legally binding in the pre-nup that says I can't?"

"No."

"Then, I *can* give it to him. You just don't want me to."

"Why would *you* want to?" he asked, furious at the thought of Cyrus taking advantage of Rowan like that.

"To get him and my family off of my back?" she asks, like it should be obvious.

"One, you can sell the property to the developer yourself which will quash my brother's interest in reconciliation." If our father's heir was only after the parcel of land. Maybe he had figured out too late what he had in Rowan and now wanted her back. "And two, curtailing Cyrus's interest in you will not stop your parents from blaming you for the breakup."

She sighed, her lips twisting with discontent. "You're right about that. And from a financial viewpoint, your first suggestion makes sense."

"Is there a viewpoint it doesn't make sense from?"

"The one where I don't need Cyrus holding a nasty grudge against me. I escaped my marriage relatively unscathed, but I'm not naïve enough to believe that Cyrus couldn't make my life here untenable if he wanted to."

"I will never allow him to hurt you." He'd been protecting her for ten years. He wasn't about to stop now.

"That's sweet, but eventually, you'll end this thing between us." She grimaced. "Or I will. And when that happens, you won't be standing as a barrier between me and your half-brother. He holds grudges."

"Never does not have an expiration date," he assured her.

He didn't know why it was so important to protect this woman, but it was a course he had committed to years ago.

She was looking at him like she had back at the table. Like he was some kind of hero. He wasn't. He was a ruthless businessman.

Having those pretty blue eyes fixed on him with that expression felt good though. So, he didn't remind her of the darker side of his nature. She'd been unwilling to see it thus far anyway.

"Okay, so we, I mean *I* sell the property to the land developer. I guess I have my lawyer approach them?"

"I will take care of it for you."

"Um, even if we were in a committed relationship, I wouldn't ask you to do that. I have a lawyer. She can take care of it."

"We agreed to exclusivity," he reminded her. "It doesn't get much more committed than that."

Giving him a teasing grin, Rowan said, "Your mom would disagree."

Despite her own life choices, or perhaps because of them, his mother would not be happy until he had bound himself legally to a woman. But that wasn't something Lysander had ever wanted to do.

It didn't make him shudder with distaste when she'd made her comments at dinner. Perhaps he was growing inured to the guilt trips.

"At the risk of sounding arrogant, I will get you a better deal than your lawyer," he said, getting back to the topic at hand.

Rowan's soft laugh affected him like it always did. Straight in his libido. But there was an odd tight feeling in his chest too. Had the food given him heartburn?

"I'm sure you can," she said with a smile. "And yes, you do sound arrogant, but it's part of your charm."

"I'll remind you that you said that the next time you aren't finding it quite so charming."

Her eyes lit with sweet humor. "You do that."

"Why do I get the feeling, you will conveniently forget this conversation?"

"Because you are a very smart man."

"Smart enough to negotiate a deal with the developer."

"Wow, you just are not going to let this go."

"I want what is best for you." In a way that would bother him if he let himself think about it. So, he didn't.

"Okay, if you really want to handle the sale, then by all means, do it."

"Tell me if Cyrus or Baptiste attempt to contact you, or threaten you in any way." He knew how vindictive both men could be, but Cyrus had a wide streak of petty as well.

"You're being bossy again."

"It's part of my charming arrogance."

"I might chalk it up to that if you charm me with another kiss."

He didn't need to be asked twice. Kissing this woman was addictive and he was greedy for another fix. Pulling her flush against his body, he let her feel what dancing with her did to him before pressing his mouth against hers.

Rowan's lips parted on a soft sigh, and he was damn tempted to ravage her mouth with his tongue. However, while he didn't care what they said about him, he did not want to give the tabloids a story to tell about her tomorrow.

Her sweet tongue came out to taste his lips and Lysander's reaction was primal and immediate. He broke the kiss and guided her from the dance floor with a firm hand at the small of her back.

"It is time to go home."

"You'll get no arguments from me," Rowan quipped.

But when they reached the table to collect her purse, Cyrus and Lysander's father were sitting in wait.

Lysander gave his father an impassive look. "Trying to poach my people?" he taunted.

"Trying to have a quiet word with my son."

Lysander usually at least listened to his father, but right then? He wanted to be home and inside his beautiful lover. "Call my assistant and make an appointment."

"Is that any way to treat your father?" Baptiste asked with a frown.

"We are leaving. If you would like to walk us out..." Lysander left the rest unsaid.

If his father wanted to talk to him that badly, he would say what he needed to between the table and the door to the outside.

Unfortunately, as soon as Baptiste stood, so did Cyrus.

Chapter Sixteen

"You must realize how badly this looks for our family," was his father's opening salvo.

Baptiste waited until they were almost to the exit doors, where few gala attendees were around to overhear the quietly spoken words. Lysander's father was more circumspect than Rowan's, but no less obvious to him.

With that sentence, Lysander knew that the property deal was not Cyrus's alone. Their father had a stake in it as well, or Andino Enterprises did. If Baptiste were genuinely concerned about the effect of his son's behavior on the family's reputation, he would have told Cyrus to keep it in his pants during his marriage to Rowan.

No, his worry was about that parcel of land, and no doubt the shares in Andino Enterprises that Rowan had been given in the divorce too. Baptiste had a vested interest in seeing Rowan and Cyrus reconciled.

Over Lysander's dead, cold and bankrupt body. No way in hell.

Lysander was not an Andino and the success of that company meant nothing to him. He couldn't care less who controlled the family shares, and he definitely had no compunction about gouging the land developer on Rowan's behalf.

Lysander did not slow his and Rowan's progress across the cavernous hotel lobby. "I disagree."

"Taking your brother's leavings as your mistress is beneath you." Baptiste's voice echoed with disgust.

Rowan stiffened beside Lysander, a soft gasp falling from her lovely mouth. Rage rolled through him with gale force.

His body stiff with fury, he stopped in the middle of the lobby, and turned to face his father and Cyrus. His brother's smarmy features looked smug, the look he gave Rowan full of superiority.

Neither Baptiste, nor Cyrus, were targeting Lysander. What they didn't seem to realize was that by aiming their vitriol at Rowan, they might as well have been.

"Do you know why my company has grown exponentially faster than Andino Enterprises in the past decade?" he asked, his tone flat.

Neither his father, nor his brother, liked that reminder and both scowled.

He did not wait to see if they would hazard a guess and answered his own question. "Because I do my research. I make sure I know my opponents before I take them on."

"I know my wife," Cyrus said scornfully. "She'll get over this little rebellion and come back to me."

"Ex-wife," Lysander gritted, the look on his face making his half-brother take a step backward.

It wasn't enough. Lysander wanted him and his father gone. He turned his sulfuric glare on his father. "I am not married. Rowan is not my mistress. She is my lover and she is nobody's leavings."

Rowan squeezed his hand. She had something she wanted to say. He refrained from adding the demand his father apologize so she could say it.

Drawing herself up, she gave the two men she'd once called family a scathing look. "Comments like that are beneath you, Baptiste. I am an independent, *single* woman who can sleep with whomever I want. And right now, I want that to be Lysander."

He didn't like the *right now* even though he had specified that their relationship would not be permanent.

Damn it. What was she doing to him?

"I apologize, Rowan," Lysander's father said stiffly.

She inclined her head regally and looked directly at her ex. "I understand why you think I'm such a pushover, Cyrus. You mistook my naivete and desire to please my parents as an indication of a lack of intelligence and weak will. Neither are attributes I carry."

"He doesn't know you at all, does he?" Lysander looked down at the magnificent woman at his side.

She held herself like a queen and her tone revealed no emotional upheaval. She had this locked down.

"No, he doesn't."

Cyrus sputtered, but slicing his hand through the air, Lysander cut his words off. "Don't bother. It's obvious you never even tried to figure out what makes Rowan tick. If you had, you would not have risked the assets assigned to her in the prenup by cheating. She's not a woman who would tolerate that. Ever."

No, his brother had assumed that because Rowan put up with their unhappy marriage, she would not balk at being cheated on. He'd completely misread her commitment to loyalty. Once he gave her an out, she was going to take it.

And she had.

"Surely that is something for Cyrus and Rowan to work through. They cannot do that if you have her in your bed." Lysander's father hissed his disapproval in a quiet tone, his attention clearly on the proximity of others and the potential for their discussion to be overheard.

"They aren't working anything out," Lysander said with bite, making no effort to modulate his own tone. "Regardless, you and Cyrus mistook my meaning. I wasn't talking about Rowan when I mentioned an opponent. I was talking about myself."

His father reeled back like Lysander had struck him. "You are my son, not my enemy."

"If you come for Rowan, I will be," he assured the older man.

"No. That's ridiculous. You don't have relationships," Cyrus said. "You're the consummate playboy." He gave Rowan a pitying look. "You must realize you are not the only woman in his bed."

"That just cost you the deal you're trying to make with the Japanese conglomerate," Lysander informed his brother. "I do not tolerate slander."

"What? How did you know about... You can't..." Cyrus stuttered.

Baptiste's expression revealed that he had finally figured out how badly he and Cyrus had messed up. "Do not be hasty, son."

If he thought calling Lysander son was going to sway the outcome, Baptiste was a fool.

"Let's make something very clear here," Lysander bit, his tone cold and threatening. "I do not care if Andino Enterprises goes bankrupt, much less loses a few million on a deal. I damn well do care if you harm someone under my protection."

"You're telling us that Rowan is under you protection?" his father asked, clearly shocked. "Since when?"

"You would know the answer to that if you had bothered to pay attention." Lysander had never been impressed with his father and brother's lazy approach to accumulating necessary information.

"She's *my* wife," Cyrus said belligerently.

"*Ex*. I'm your *ex*-wife," Rowan piped up with that reminder, emphasizing the ex. "I haven't lived with you for over a year. The divorce is final. I changed my name back to Johnson. We're as over as over can be."

Cyrus and Baptiste looked at Rowan with twin expressions of consternation. Baptiste's gaze turned considering, but anger tightened Cyrus's face.

"I know you're a petty, vindictive man, Cyrus," Rowan said, showing she knew her ex much better than he'd ever known her. "Refrain from trying to get back at me for having the audacity to divorce your cheating ass, or I will sign my shares in Andino Enterprises over to your biggest competition."

"You're not giving shares in *my* company to that bastard," Cyrus shouted, pointing at Lysander.

Baptiste grabbed his legitimate son's arm in warning.

Rowan laughed, the sound more mockery than humor. "You think you're in competition with Lysander? You're not even in the same stratosphere. He doesn't need shares in Andino Enterprises to crush it."

Her words filled Lysander with unexpected pride. Not only did she know more about his business than his so-called family, but she recognized the financial power he wielded.

His reaction to her approval was disconcerting though. It was too intense.

"Who are you talking about then?" The snide condescension rolled off his half-brother.

Rowan named the company Lysander himself considered most likely to launch a hostile merger attempt on Andino Enterprises if they were able to add a block of the company's shares to their portfolio.

"Lysander, you may not be part of Andino Enterprises, but you are still my son. You owe family loyalty." His father sounded almost desperate.

Was Andino Enterprises in trouble financially? Why else would Baptiste and Cyrus be so fixated on bringing the shares and the land parcel back into their greedy little hands?

Rowan had had a point earlier. Why hadn't they simply offered to buy them from her?

It was something he needed to look into.

"The only family I owe loyalty to is my mother." He was a Baros, not an Andino as Cyrus had so eloquently pointed out when he called Lysander a bastard. "The woman you disrespected by taking to your bed but not the altar when you had the chance."

His father winced, eyes so like Lysander's own, going bleak.

Perhaps Rowan had been right, and the older man *had* grieved for the loss of Iona Baros. However, that loss was entirely his own doing. Lysander had no sympathy for Baptiste or his regrets.

Nor did he feel unswerving loyalty toward him. Yes, Baptiste had acknowledged Lysander as his *illegitimate* son, but in many ways that had only made Lysander's life more difficult in the predominately conservative business world of Athens.

His father had never attempted to bring Lysander into the family business or his own life in any meaningful way. Expecting loyalty to a family name that Lysander did not carry was ludicrous.

If Baptiste did not want to lose his company, he had better keep a tighter rein on Cyrus as Rowan's ex than he had when he was her husband. If Rowan didn't bring them down by selling her shares to their keenest competitor, Lysander would take the company apart piece by piece.

Dismantling the deal with the Japanese conglomerate would show both men how serious Lysander was about keeping and protecting Rowan.

He'd meant his promise to her earlier. Even after their liaison ended, Lysander would keep Cyrus's revenge impulses in check where she was concerned.

"Marriage is a sacred institution," his father said, trying another tack.

Lysander gave the older man a disbelieving look. "You are saying this to me? The result of you not keeping your *sacred* vows to your first wife."

Rowan's hand squeezed his. She was trying to comfort him. He did not need it. He'd long since come to terms with his own origin story. The gesture warmed him though.

She was just so damn sweet.

"You don't want me back," Rowan said to Cyrus, with unwavering conviction. "This is all about what I got in the divorce settlement. Newsflash, you aren't getting any of it back."

She'd gone from wanting to just give him the parcel of land to refusing to give him anything. Rowan had a temper that spurred intransigence, as he had learned the day she'd shown up at his gate with her intriguing proposition.

Rowan rolled her eyes when Cyrus's face went slack with shock, and she shook her head. "Did you really think I would be fooled a second time by your attempt at romance? How gullible do you think I am?"

"I don't know what Lysander has told you, Rowan, but keep in mind that he has an axe to grind with our family."

Lysander was done.

Rowan's feisty side turned him on, and he'd already been aroused by their dancing. His tuxedo jacket was hiding a raging hardon he was ready to bury in his lover's enticing body.

As if she could read his mind, or maybe her body was reacting to his pheromones, Rowan looked up at him with a sultry smile. "Time to go, don't you think, Sander?"

"Yes," he growled.

Chapter Seventeen

The sexual tension in the car on the way back to Lysander's home was palpable. Rowan pressed her thighs together trying to alleviate the ache between them.

It did not work.

Lysander gripped the steering wheel with white-knuckle intensity. "Why didn't I use a driver tonight?"

"Because you like handling this super expensive, finely tuned machine?" she teased.

"I like handling you more."

"I'm flattered. I think."

"You should be. You're the only woman in that category."

"I guess I'm special then."

His gaze flicked sideways to her before returning to the road. "You are that."

They barely made it through the front door before they were tearing off each other's clothing. Rowan ran her hands over the hard plains of his chest, reveling in her freedom to touch this sexy man however she liked.

His hands gripped tightly around her hips, he lifted her against the wall in the foyer and took her mouth forcefully.

Rowan gave back as good as she got, tangling her tongue with his, spreading her legs so the juncture of her thighs rubbed against the hard ridges of his eight-pack. She was so wet, it soaked right through her panties and made his skin slick.

He dropped her legs and jerked her panties down. She kicked off her shoes and stepped out of her underwear while he yanked her dress over her head. Then she stood naked because she hadn't been wearing a bra.

With a groan, Lysander brought his mouth down to her breast and he laved her peaked nipple. "So sweet," he breathed against her sensitive flesh.

"Please, Sander...I *need*."

He maneuvered her a couple of feet to the right and then she found herself perched on the edge of a console table while his raging erection pressed against her most intimate flesh.

"Yes." She wanted this. So much. "Put it in me."

He surged forward, his huge manhood getting stuck after only a couple of inches despite how ready she was.

Pulling back and thrusting forward in short jabs, he worked more of his hard penis inside her swollen channel. "So damn tight."

She tried to help, but she had no traction with her legs dangling off the side of the console table.

Finally, the root of his sex pressed against her vulva. A mini starburst of pleasure went through her. And then he started to thrust for real, pistoning in and out of her body in an uncontrolled rhythm that quickly brought her to the brink of ecstasy.

His pelvis pressed against her clitoris with every forward thrust and that ecstasy flooded her in a tsunami of feeling.

Her head tilted back, she screamed with an abandon she couldn't hope to leash.

Lysander stopped thrusting, just grinding his pelvis against her to prolong her bliss.

He stared down at her, his face tight with need. "You are so beautiful like this."

Then he started canting his hips again and soon his big, muscled body went rigid with his own climax. His shout was loud and guttural.

But recognizable for all that.

He'd yelled her name as he came.

Something cracked inside of Rowan. Something she had no desire to acknowledge or examine.

~ ~ ~

Blissful days turned into blissful weeks, and Rowan realized she'd been living with Lysander for two months.

With no signs of either of them growing bored with the other's company.

And the sex was hot and plentiful.

It was almost too good to be true and Rowan kept waiting for Lysander to change. To start treating her like a piece of furniture as Cyrus had done. As she had seen so many men in her life do to their society wives.

Maybe it was because she was his lover and not his wife, but Lysander wanted to talk over dinner. He cajoled her into getting up ridiculously early so they could have breakfast together before he left for the office.

They had dinner with his mother and her husband. Rowan met Lysander's business associates because he liked having her with him when they had a dinner meeting.

She got to know his staff and security specialists, but she still called them goons so they wouldn't grow complacent.

She was in danger of growing more than complacent; she was becoming attached. To Lysander. To his life. To the life they shared together.

~ ~ ~

Upon her return to the villa after work, Rowan was surprised to find Lysander home as well. He relaxed on the leather sectional in his inner sanctum, the television showing the stock markets somewhere, his tablet in his hand.

It was so like that first day she'd come here, she smiled. "You're back early."

He swiped and tapped something on his tablet and put it down. Looking up at her, his dark eyes heated. "And you are late."

"Couldn't be helped." Though if she'd known he was already here, she would have tried harder to leave on time.

He stood and put his hand out. "You are here now. Come."

"Are we having sex for dinner again?" she asked, tongue in cheek.

"Have I ever let you skip a meal?"

"No." He was kind of militant about making sure she got dinner, even if it was in bed after making love.

"Helen packed for you, but you'll want to check and make sure she got everything you'll need."

"Are we going somewhere?" It was Friday. So, they had the weekend. Or at least she did. Lysander almost always had to work at least part of the weekend.

It took a lot of effort to stay at the top of the tycoon food chain.

"We are going on a cruise."

Excitement made Rowan's blood bubble in her veins like champagne. "A weekend cruise?"

It wasn't Mexico, but it was a cruise. And he'd booked it for her. If she didn't watch out, she was going to fall head over heels for this man.

"We'll be spending ten days in the Mexican Riviera."

Rowan stopped walking, her heart thudding. She stared up at Lysander, certain she'd misheard him. "What did you say?"

"You want to go on a cruise in Mexico." His tone and expression said he was still confused as to why.

"Yes, so?"

"So, we are going. I've spoken to Ariston Spiridakou. He owns a cruise line and has provided accommodation on one of his luxury ships."

Rowan couldn't even fathom what level of opulence would cause a contemporary of Lysander to refer to the vessel as a *luxury* ship.

"No way are you taking ten days away from work."

Lysander shrugged. "I will work remotely for a couple of hours a day. I can take conference calls as necessary."

That sounded more like her workaholic lover, but still. "I can't just take off for vacation without making sure everything is covered at work."

"Taken care of."

"What do you mean?"

"I contacted your org's director. She okayed your absence."

"But we're in the middle of a fund-raising push."

"A couple of my people will be filling in for you."

"You think of everything."

Chapter Eighteen

Rowan realized how true that statement was as she found herself on a private jet flying toward Los Angeles, California. The Greek cruise line embarked from the Port of Los Angeles.

Lysander had arranged for her things to be packed, very efficiently, by Helen. He'd ordered dinner to be served on board the plane. But best of all, he had an entire itinerary with shore excursions for her to pore over.

"Choose the ones you want to go on and I'll have them booked for us."

"You're going on a group shore excursion?" Rowan couldn't help the surprise in her tone. "*You* are?"

"No." His gorgeous smile slashed across his face. "We will have private guides and transportation."

Of course, they would.

After selecting the places and things she wanted to see and do in each cruise port, Rowan stared at Lysander and wondered how long it would take him to feel her eyes on him. It was no hardship.

Her Greek tycoon lover was gorgeous. And that look he got on his face when he was concentrating on work? It made her heart rat-a-tat-tat and her panties damp. He was just so sexy in his king-of-the-business-world mode.

Was it the intelligence shining in his dark eyes as he read through reports? Or maybe how incongruous his perfectly sculpted body was to his tycoon role. Billionaires were just *not* this gorgeous. The proof was in every business journal and tabloid on the planet.

Most of those men were at least a decade older than Lysander and none of them had his rugged good looks. At least in her opinion. Which might be biased.

Is that what love did to you?

Rowan's brain screeched to a silent halt like an incomplete music download. Love? Who said anything about love?

She could not love this man. That emotion was strictly off limits in their temporary relationship.

Lysander looked up from the email he'd been writing to one of his subsidiary CEOs and found Rowan staring at him like she'd seen a paparazzi outside the plane window. Disbelief tinged with disgust dominated her beautiful face.

It was not the expression he expected to see after she'd been going over their itinerary options for Mexico.

"What is the matter? Is there an excursion you find distasteful?"

Shaking herself, Rowan's expression cleared. "No. They're all great. It was hard to choose, if you want the truth."

"I always want the truth from you."

She winced and then shook her head. "Pretty sure you don't."

"I do." He had no doubts on that score.

"Do you have a lot more work to do?" she asked. "Only, I thought we might make use of the bedroom. I've never been on a private jet with one before."

"Are you tired?" he teased.

Rowan's libido easily matched his. No way was she talking about sleeping.

"Not so much, no." Whatever had put the distressed look on her face wasn't at the forefront of her mind now.

Sex was. And just like that, it was the overriding thought in his brain too.

He shut his laptop and set it aside before standing. Putting his hand out to Rowan, he said, "Let's go see how comfortable the bed is."

"You don't know?"

"No."

"Why have a bed on your plane if you don't use it?" she asked with a tilt of her head, her expression curious and little judgy. "I know you aren't keen on sleeping more than a few hours a night, but even you must rest on the longer trips."

She was right on both counts. He didn't require much sleep, but using travel time to get what he did need was only logical. "It is not my plane."

Surprise widened her lovely blue eyes. "It isn't?"

"It belongs to a friend." He had considered how much he wanted to say to her, but Lysander had decided that she would want to know the full truth. "I did not want our travel arrangements easily tracked."

"What? Why not?"

"The threats have escalated and now include you." The anger and tension that had simmered inside him since being made aware of her name being mentioned in the latest threat threatened to boil over.

"You didn't say anything."

"I'm saying something now."

"I guess you are." She chewed on her lip. "You wouldn't be leaving if it wasn't for me being threatened, would you?"

"No." A man in his position received threats too often to let them dictate even a modest change to his schedule.

Having her targeted changed things.

"So, we're flying incognito?"

"We are not listed by name on the flight manifest."

"Is that legal?"

"No."

"Oh."

He didn't want her frightened. "My security company has a plan for smoking out the culprits."

"That's good."

"I wanted you out of Europe while they do it."

"And you came with me to keep me company? You could have just sent me on the cruise alone."

That was not going to happen.

"The look on your face. Are you worried I'd flirt with the other guests on board?"

"No." He was understandably concerned a woman as beautiful and vivacious as she was would get hit on by other men. "As long as we are together, we are exclusive."

"That's what we agreed."

"Then there is nothing to be concerned about."

"And yet, here you are, flying anonymously on a plane to another country in order to go on a cruise with me." She shook her head, disbelief etched on her face. "That whole incognito thing, it seems really cloak and dagger."

"It is a little. Body doubles will be living in the villa, pretending to be us while we are away." The fully trained security agents would be engaging in activity meant to draw the threat out into the open.

"This really is a working vacation for you. Can I expect to see much of you at all on the cruise?" she asked, disappointment clear in her drooped shoulders.

"Yes. I said I would only work a couple of hours a day. You don't think I'm sending you ashore alone, do you?" Like hell.

Not only would he be with her, but they were traveling with a full complement of security.

"I'm glad you aren't." She grinned, her natural enthusiasm coming to the fore. "I'm surprised you didn't just plan for us to visit one of your company headquarters outside Europe."

"You wanted to go on a cruise. To Mexico." And he wanted to see her eyes light up the way they had when he told her about their trip.

"So, you got in touch with one of your Greek tycoon friends who just happens to own a luxury cruise line?"

"Ariston is more a business associate than a friend." Lysander didn't have friends. He had family, some of whom he would happily live without.

His father. His brother.

One he cared deeply about. His mother. Others he considered important because his mother did. Her relatives.

But friends? No.

"Are we traveling under assumed names?" Rowan's voice was laced with excitement.

He chuckled. "Nothing so mysterious. I'm sorry, but I don't have a fake passport for you, or any super spy gadgets."

She gave him a moue of regret. "It is a little disappointing."

"I'll make up for it," he promised.

"You can start back there." She tilted her head toward the bedroom in the back of the plane.

Arousal whooshed through him in a heated wave. "Yes, let's test the firmness of the bed."

"If it's anything like your bed at the villa, I'm sure it's as firm as can be."

"Are you saying my bed at home is too hard for you?"

"Nothing about you is *too* hard," she teased in a low, sultry voice. "Your hardness is just right."

Then she jumped up and rushed to the back of the plane, her laughter trailing behind her.

Cheeky minx.

He would show her just how hard she made him and he could only hope the bed would withstand his efforts.

~ ~ ~

There were three cruise ships docked when Rowan and Lysander reached the harbor. The one owned by Ariston Spiridakou gleamed pristinely white in the sunshine. It wasn't quite as large as the other two ships and she just knew that meant it was because fewer guests were accommodated, not because it lacked any amenity.

Fizzing with excitement, she clutched her hold all on one side of her body and Lysander's hand on the other. "I can't believe you made this happen. Thank you, Sander."

"My pleasure." He laced their fingers and pulled her close as they walked toward the ship.

No passport or check-in lines for men like Lysander Baros. Their security detail surrounded them and handed over all necessary documents to ship personal.

"Where are all of the other passengers?" she asked the purser, who was personally escorting them to their cabin.

"General boarding does not begin for three hours."

Of course.

He ushered them through a door marked *cruise personnel*. It led to a surprisingly well appointed corridor with an elevator in the center.

"This is your personal elevator," the purser explained. "It is accessible via doors in the same position on every deck and requires your keycard and thumbprint to call."

It sounded like excessive security measures to reach their cabin, but this was the world of a billionaire. The purser left them at the elevator after scanning both their thumbprints and giving them each a keycard with their pictures on them.

She'd read that the card with their picture was used as identification to get on and off the ship, but again, Rowan doubted it worked that way for friends of the owner of the cruise line.

When the elevator doors opened, Lysander held Rowan back from exiting. All but one of their security detail did though. "This is their suite."

From the glimpse Rowan got through the open doors, the suite had a large living area with four doors off of it. The security specialists' rooms?

But her curiosity about the sleeping arrangements for their guards disintegrated into nothingness when she saw their suite. "This place is bigger than my apartment back in Athens. I thought cabins on cruise ships were supposed to be small."

She'd expected a suite and more space than the typical cabin. She was traveling with Lysander Baros after all, but this? This was over the top luxury and space.

The security specialist did his thing making sure the rooms off the main living area were empty. "All clear, Mr. Baros," he said.

Lysander nodded. "Make sure at least two men are available at all times to guard Rowan and I if we leave the suite."

The man nodded and left via the elevator.

"Pfft," Rowan said. "This isn't a suite. It's a luxury apartment."

Lysander's brows rose. "Is that a complaint?"

"You know it's not. This is amazing." She twirled and indicated the beautifully appointed space with her hands out.

Lysander grabbed her by the waist and pulled her in. Like he couldn't help but touch her. "It is Ariston and Chloe's personal accommodation."

"They keep a palatial suite like this on all their ships?" Wow. Just, wow.

"Not all."

"More than one though?"

He nodded, his eyes fixed on her lips.

"But..." Talk about excess.

"It is good to be king."

"Says one monarch about another."

Her *king* bent and pressed his mouth to hers in a kiss that quickly turned carnal.

Rowan was breathing hard when he lifted his head and stared down at her with an expression she couldn't begin to read. "You are too damn addicting."

"Pot, meet kettle," she teased.

But he didn't smile. Shaking his head, he stepped away. "Come and see the balcony."

Lysander tugged Rowan toward a huge sliding glass door that led outside. The balcony was huge, covering the entire width of their suite. With lounge furniture and a large hot tub to the left, as well as a family size table for outdoor dining to the right, it was easily as large as one of the terraces off Lysander's villa.

They were on the top deck of the ship with a 280° view around them. The wall surrounding the balcony was clear, which surprised her.

"I would think someone like Ariston Spiridakou would be more intent on his privacy."

Lysander pressed a button on the wall by the door and the walls around the terrace went frosted and opaque.

"Ooh, clever." She stepped into Lysander's personal space. "I can think of something we could do with the privacy."

Lysander took a step back, away from her. "I need to do some work as long as we're in port. Why don't you get settled?"

He disappeared inside the suite.

CHAPTER NINETEEN

Doing her best to ignore the sting of the rejection, Rowan went back inside too.

She wasn't anywhere near done exploring.

Lysander had said he would have to work a couple of hours each day and there hadn't been much time for it this morning. They'd landed at a private airstrip outside of Los Angeles and then been driven to the port.

He'd spent some time on his phone in the car, but she was sure he needed some privacy to make calls and whatever else tycoons did to fill their work hours. Of which there were many.

Opening one door, Rowan found a small but well appointed bathroom with a shower. The next two doors, on either side of the bathroom revealed small bedrooms. Across the living area, there were only two doors.

She could hear the muffled tones of Lysander's voice behind one and assumed that was some kind of office. She doubted Ariston was any great shakes about taking time off from his mega empire either. The next room was a master bedroom complete with an en suite with both a full separate tub and shower.

This place was *bigger* than her apartment in Athens, by a bedroom, an office and at least 50% more living space in the main room. There was no kitchen, but then on a cruise ship, she assumed there was no need for one. There was a small fridge and fully stocked personal bar area.

This place was set up to accommodate a family. Did Ariston and Chloe travel with their family? She didn't know much about the other Greek tycoon. Not even his age. For all she knew, their children were grown, but Rowan still felt a twinge in her chest when she thought about traveling like this with children.

It wasn't the opulence surrounding her that had her feeling wistful. It was the idea of having children. Something she hadn't wanted after the first year in her marriage to Cyrus.

What would Lysander's child be like? Willful and stubborn, for sure. She could see a little boy with his father's intense dark eyes in her mind's eye.

Pushing thoughts better left to old and buried dreams, Rowan strolled over to the dining table.

In the center of it, a platter of fruit and cheese tempted her. Sitting next to it was a bucket with a bottle of champagne chilling in the ice. She read the note beside it:

Lysander & Rowan:

Enjoy your trip. My staff has been instructed to get you whatever you need.

Ariston

Short and to the point, but a nice touch all the same.

Now, if only she had a lover to share the champagne with. Drinking bubbly on her own was not exactly Rowan's norm. Especially this early in the day.

She grabbed a bunch of grapes to nibble on and wandered outside again. The sounds of the cruise port were muted, but still discernable from her place on the top deck. The hot tub made a sound, like it was running a routine filtration cycle.

Hmm...nothing was stopping her from putting on her bikini and availing herself of the warm bubbly water.

She wanted to watch the ship leave port, but that would not be for hours yet. Who knew how many of those hours Lysander would spend holed up in the suite's study?

Putting thought to action, she hurried into the bedroom and opened her suitcase. She could unpack. That was probably what Lysander meant by settling in, but the hot tub beckoned. And unlike her temporary lover, Rowan was not a workaholic.

Unplanned, or not, this was her vacation and she meant to enjoy every minute of it.

A couple of minutes later, after changing into her swimsuit and pulling her hair into a messy bun, Rowan padded out barefoot to the balcony. Not wanting anything to impede her view, she pressed the button turning the glass back to clear.

The water was hot, but not too hot and Rowan let her body sink onto a seat under the bubbles. She had an unimpeded view of the harbor and watched boats coming and going. The suite was on the stern of the ship, so all she saw on the deck two stories below was an empty outdoor eating area.

When the ship was full, she was sure it was busy and was grateful for the option to turn the glass opaque. Maybe she was too spoiled by her lifestyle to truly enjoy a regular cruise with regular people, but the idea of being watched while she relaxed felt like nails on a chalkboard to her brain.

This was perfect though. And she *did* want to eat in the public restaurants. She wanted to play trivia with the other guests in the bar area. And take dance lessons on the pool deck. Rowan had read about all these activities and more when she'd looked into taking a cruise by herself.

She'd never worked up the enthusiasm to travel alone though.

Being here with Lysander was perfect. Well, it would be when he wasn't working. Which she wasn't going to complain about. Not even to herself. She wasn't about to become a vine and cling either. Not her style.

So, if participating in onboard activities meant doing it alone, that's what Rowan would do. She couldn't help hoping she'd convince Lysander to join her at least part of the time, though.

She thought she was in with a chance. Lysander had tried things with her he hadn't done before. Like moving her into his home. She was the only woman he'd ever lived with besides his mother.

That meant something, didn't it?

More importantly, what did she want it to mean?

When this thing between them first started, she had been no more interested in commitment than he was, certain her emotions were locked down tight. Feeling bereft when he chose to work rather than make love? That said otherwise.

Sure, she could pretend to herself it was all about sexual frustration, but she didn't make it a habit to lie to herself like that. And she wasn't going to start now.

Their relationship had a sell by date and while she'd wanted that to start with, now it felt like the Sword of Damocles hanging over her head.

Neither of them knew what that date was, and she was sure Lysander didn't spend a single second worrying about it. However, the inevitable end of their liaison was starting to color their time together in shades of grief she couldn't let herself show.

She didn't even know which one of them would end it. Because it could be her. No matter how much she craved him in her life, she might walk away to protect herself from further pain.

Since that first dance they'd shared, she'd felt a connection to Lysander she'd never known with another man. While married she hadn't acted on that feeling, or even allowed herself to dwell on it. No secret fantasies of a man she wasn't married to.

Unlike Cyrus, Rowan was loyal. And she believed in keeping her word. Even if that meant letting go of a man she wasn't sure she could live happily without when the time came.

It was time to stop pretending she'd approached him with her plan solely in order to get rid of her ex-husband's attention.

Rowan had dressed up like an amateur seductress and gone to Lysander because she wanted him. Full stop. Having had him...over and over again for the past weeks...she only wanted him more.

Far from working him out of her system, he had worked his way into the fortress that had been her heart.

The only man on the planet who could.

And she'd been the fool to come to him, to suggest they have revenge sex that turned into the most intimate and fulfilling sex of her life.

"What are you doing out here?" Lysander barked.

Rowan jerked in surprise, slipping from her perch on the molded seat below her and sputtered as water splashed up into her face.

She'd been so lost in her thoughts, she hadn't heard him approach.

Allowing the momentum from her slide into the water to propel her, she floated to the side of the hot tub. Settling her crossed arms on it, she lifted her head and gave him a wry glance. "I think that's pretty obvious, yeah?"

"It sure as hell is." He jabbed the button turning the glass of the surround frosted once again. "I don't want men leering at you in your bikini."

"So possessive," she teased.

She should probably at least put up a token resistance to such blatant jealousy, but it secretly thrilled her. He wanted her to be his and his alone. Even the right to look at her swimsuit clad body. At least for now.

Not that she was giving up public swimming, but she liked the way his over-the-top reaction made her feel.

"Are you done working?" she asked with an inviting smile. "Only, it's a little lonely in this hot tub."

"How can you be lonely when you're displaying your body for anyone to see?"

Okay. No matter how much this version of her lover turned her on, enough was enough.

"Newsflash, we are on a cruise ship, Sander. There will be other men by the pool when we use it. I can't stop them leering, though I doubt I'll be the only woman down there in a bikini." She put her hand up in a stop gesture when Lysander looked like he wanted to speak. She waived toward the outdoor dining area two decks below. "And there are no people down there right now."

"We won't be using the pool when other guests have access to it," Lysander dismissed.

"Maybe you won't, but I'm not spending the entire day holed up in the suite while you are working."

He looked taken aback by her words, like it had never occurred to him that she would explore what the ship had to offer without him.

"That is not acceptable."

"It's cute how you think you get to dictate to me, but here's another bit of news, Mr. Greek tycoon, you aren't the boss of me."

Chapter Twenty

"I thought it was King?"

"I'm American. We don't do sovereigns."

"You chose to have a life in Greece."

"Greece abolished the monarchy in 1974." Her words said one thing, her mind another. Because Lysander had the presence and bearing of royalty.

He began unbuttoning his shirt, his suit jacket and tie nowhere in evidence.

"What are you doing?" she parroted his question.

He gave her a look that asked what she thought he was doing because it should be obvious. "Undressing so I can join you."

"You're not wearing swim trunks under your slacks. I saw you get dressed."

"Nor do I need them in a private spa."

"Oh." She wasn't sure why a small piece of clothing made a difference, but it did.

The idea of him sliding into the hot tub naked made her core pulse. She pressed her thighs together to alleviate the ache, but all that did was make her more aware of what she wanted.

Him. His hands there. His sex *there*.

The predatory look in his eye was like a brush straight over her clitoris.

Peeling out of his clothes, soon Lysander stood naked and proud, the sun shining on his tanned skin and sculpted muscles.

"Corporate sharks shouldn't look so much like ancient Greek gods," she muttered.

His laughter said he'd heard her. "From a king to a god, what is next?"

She didn't answer, too busy watching him walk toward her, his sex already half mast. His defined muscles bunching with each movement of his legs.

"You look like you're ready to eat me," he said, a sexy smile slashing across his face.

What that tone and look did to her. She had no hope of nonchalance in the face of such masculine beauty and strength.

Sexual hunger washed over her.

Rowan was not complaining. Not even a little. She reveled in the way her body responded to him.

"Getting my mouth on you sounds about right," Rowan said throatily.

Only this man brought out the Siren in her.

Eschewing the handrail and steps, he lifted one long powerful leg over the side and turned, bringing the rest of his lower body into contact with the water. But he didn't sink under.

Instead, he sat on the side, and indicated his now fully erect length with his hand. "Have at it."

He didn't need to ask her twice. Rowan's mouth watered for a taste of him. She turned and propelled herself across the hot tub, only stopping when she was between his knees.

Kneading his hard thighs with her hands, she said, "Don't mind if I do."

Leaning forward, she nuzzled into the skin between his hip and his torso. Taking a deep inhalation of his masculine scent, Rowan exulted in her right to this intimacy no other woman was allowed.

For now.

Ignoring the sting of that reminder, she took in the hint of the sandalwood soap he used in the shower mixed with the distinctly intimate fragrance of his skin here. This amazing god of a man was hers.

However temporarily. Right now? His body was her playground. And she meant to play to her heart's content.

She bit gently on his inner thigh and then laved the spot with her tongue. He groaned and she smiled to herself before turning her head to do the same to his other leg. She was oh so careful not to touch his balls or his hard shaft.

His big hands gripped her on either side of her head. "What you do to me, *yineka mou*."

His woman. Oh, she liked when he called her that. Way too much.

Until one of them said otherwise, she was his. Just like he was hers.

Mouthing along his skin she traveled down his rock hard thigh toward his knee before making the reverse journey up his other leg. She stopped with her mouth pressed against his groin and kissed him there.

With a sound of sexual frustration and desire, his hips canted upward.

She loved teasing him, pushing him to the limit of his vaunted self-control. Loved even more when she managed to shove him right over into pure animal lust.

Right now, she didn't want him taking over though, so she slid her lips toward his sex. Dipping her head so she could lick delicately at his scrotum, she rubbed her cheek against his erection.

~ ~ ~

Of their own volition, Lysander's fingers tunneled through Rowan's silky hair. He was not at all disappointed when the tie that held it on top of her head in a messy bun was dislodged.

Her hair fell around her face and shoulders in a silky red curtain, brushing over his thighs like a mass of butterfly wings. The soft skin of her cheek brushed against his fully erect cock while she licked at his aching balls.

It all felt so damn good, but he wanted more.

Why had he rejected her sexual overture earlier? There had been nothing in his inbox so damn important it could not wait.

When he realized he was hiding from her and the way she made him feel, he'd told himself to man up and go claim his woman.

Only now, she was claiming him.

Sensually. Perfectly. Irrevocably.

Ignoring the implication of that last thought, he directed her head up so her mouth was right there. Warm air puffed over the head of his dick, her lips only millimeters away.

Heavy lidded, her beautiful blue eyes teased him with sensual promise. "Do you want something?"

"Your mouth on me," he said in a guttural voice.

This woman drove him to the brink of his restraint. She licked up and down his turgid pole, kissing the head with an open mouth, but not taking him inside her wet heat.

"What are you doing to me?" he demanded.

In answer, she grasped him in her wet hand and pulled along his length. It wasn't enough.

"I want your mouth."

"Then take it." She opened her lips wide, but left her mouth poised at the end of his cock, her gaze challenging him.

His grip on her head tightened and he pulled her face forward, lust riding him, but he watched for any sign this wasn't what she wanted. She gave none, flicking her tongue out to lick the pearls of precum gathering on the end of his dick.

Pushing forward, he tugged her onto his cock and she hummed with approval, but she didn't move her head. What did she want?

Her hands came up and gripped his. She tugged, directing him to guide her. A wildfire of lust burned through his control and he pushed to the back of her mouth. When he touched her throat, she didn't gag, but swallowed, pulling him deeper and he was lost.

He thrust in and out of her mouth, the sounds of arousal she made around his thick flesh increasing his need until he was nearly mindless with it.

"I'm going to come," he warned her.

Her hands gripped his harder while she sucked and swallowed. Ecstasy exploded in a cataclysm of pleasure as he shot his ejaculate down her throat. Everything in his brain went white, his body transported by a level of rapturous pleasure he'd never experienced with anyone else.

Only this woman.

She licked him clean as she pulled her head backward and then turned to nuzzle into his hand.

That small act of affection set his libido right back to overdrive. He grabbed her waist and yanked her up until their lips came together in harsh passion. She wrapped her arms around his neck and kissed him back with violent fervor.

Surging up, he brought her body with his and she wrapped her legs around him. Somehow, he got them out of the hot tub and into the bedroom and he laid her on the bed, uncaring about the water from her body soaking the duvet.

"You are beautiful in this, but even more gorgeous out of it." He tugged her bikini bottoms down her legs.

Rowan lifted up on her elbows, giving him easy access to the clasps on her top's straps, but made no move to take it off herself.

It took him only seconds to undo both the neck and back straps so he could pull the wet and clinging fabric away from her generous mounds. His mouth watered as nipples beaded and flushed with arousal were revealed to his eyes.

He dove down and took one of those tempting little gems into his mouth, sucking and nipping while he kneaded the fleshy mound around it. His dick was still hard despite shooting like a geyser down Rowan's throat. Nudging her thighs apart, he rubbed his hard flesh against her wet folds and clitoris.

Moaning, she thrashed beneath him and splayed her legs wider in invitation.

Surging up her body, he took her mouth as he invaded her. Rowan's slick wetness allowed him to seat himself in her tight channel in a single hard thrust.

She cried out and he stilled.

Squirming against him, she broke the kiss. "Don't you dare stop, Sander. It's too good."

The words were all the permission he needed to start pounding into her. He had no intention of stopping until they were both wrung out from pleasure. She climaxed quickly, but he was nowhere near done with her.

He pulled out only to renew his attack on her senses with his mouth and hands. He'd wrung three orgasms out of her before he pushed his now throbbing cock deep inside her and brought them both to a final climax that was a near out of body experience.

~ ~ ~

Rowan didn't know what had come over Lysander, but there was no hope of leaving their suite to explore the cruise ship that first night. He kept them both naked and played her body like the sexual virtuoso he was, building her arousal and need over and over again.

She woke the next morning with a delicious ache between her legs and a not so delicious one in her lower back. She groaned as she went to sit up, the bed beside her empty.

No surprise there. Lysander rarely stayed in bed until she woke.

After going to the bathroom, Rowan slipped a sleeveless t-shirt dress over her nakedness and gingerly made her way into the main room.

Lysander sat at the dining table, his computer in front of him and a cup of coffee off to the side.

His eyes narrowed on her. "What's wrong?"

"Nothing. I'm just a little sore from all our calisthenics yesterday."

Jumping up from the table, he crossed the room in a few long strides. "Sore? Where? Did I hurt you?"

"No, Sander, you did not hurt me." She reached up, offering her lips for a kiss.

Which he took. Gently.

She smiled. "You gave me a surfeit of pleasure. My muscles just aren't used to the exercise."

"You haven't been like this before," he said, accusingly.

"We tried a couple of positions we haven't before. Both of which I enjoyed very much by the way." She'd lost count of her orgasms long before they fell into exhausted slumber in each other's arms. "After breakfast, I'll have a soak in the hot tub."

Which sounded way too good. Maybe hot tub first and breakfast after.

Lysander shook his head. "I'll get you some pain reliever and order a massage for you."

"Ooh, I can't wait to see the spa. I bet it's gorgeous on a ship like this."

"You won't be going to the spa." He walked toward the bedroom. "They will come here."

"There's no point in being on a cruise ship if I spend all of my time while at sea in this suite," she called to his retreating back.

Not waiting for him to reply, she picked up the phone and ordered some breakfast.

Lysander returned from the bedroom and held out two gel caps. Rowan took them gratefully and the glass of water he offered with them.

Tossing the pain relievers into the back of her mouth, she took a gulp of water to swallow them down. Then she picked up the phone receiver again and pressed the button to connect to the spa.

A chipper voice said, "Serenity. What can we do for you today, Mrs. Baros."

Rowan flushed hot all over at being called Mrs. Baros, but didn't correct the other woman. She didn't know if it had been a mistake or if the suite was booked under Mr. and Mrs. Lysander Baros.

"I would like to book a massage sometime today if that's possible."

"Of course, but we can send a masseuse to your suite if you'd rather."

Was this a conspiracy, or something? "That won't be necessary. I prefer to come there for the service."

"Of course, Mrs. Baros."

They finalized the details for the massage while Lysander stood glowering beside her. "I don't like you wandering the ship on your own."

"I very much doubt I'll be alone. Unless you aren't planning to have the security specialists shadow me like they do back in Athens?" she asked hopefully.

"No chance."

"Then I'll hardly be *wandering the ship on my own*, will I?" She rolled her eyes. Billionaires. They didn't see the world like regular people.

"I would prefer to be with you when you leave the suite."

"No." She wasn't hanging around in the suite all day while he worked. "Not going to happen."

"You do not want to spend time with me?" he asked. "You were keen enough for my company yesterday."

Rowan blushed at the reminder of how ardent she'd been in their lovemaking.

"But then we were having sex," he continued, his dark brow raised. "Weren't you the one who said this relationship had to be about more than sex if you were going to move in with me?"

"Let me clarify. I'm happy for you to join me whenever you have the time to do so, but I will not limit my expeditions outside of the suite to those times."

"Call Serenity back and book a couples massage."

"You want to get a massage too?" she asked.

"I would prefer doing so in the comfort of our suite."

Rowan sighed. "All right. I'll ask them to come here."

"You want to go to the spa." His tone was the same as when he'd acknowledged she wanted to go on a cruise.

He didn't understand why she wanted it, but he was willing to indulge her.

She hoped.

Rowan looked at Lysander appealingly. "Yes."

"Then book our couples massage at Serenity."

"They might not have another masseuse available," she warned. "I read that days at sea are busy for the spa and other onboard services."

"They will accommodate us, Rowan."

"Because we are staying in the private suite of the owner of the cruise line," she guessed, feeling silly for even doubting they would make room in their schedule for her and/or Lysander.

"Perhaps, but the room is booked in my name."

And billionaire tycoon Lysander Baros was kind of a big deal.

"You really want to get a couple's massage with me?" she asked.

"Yes."

Unable to help the grin spreading over her face, Rowan called Serenity again and made the arrangements. Lysander checked his phone while she was talking to the receptionist.

"Klaus will be up momentarily with your breakfast," he said after she put the handset down.

"Not a steward?"

"No one but our security staff and the approved cleaning staff while in their company will be allowed into the suite."

And apparently staff from the spa if they so desired. She'd bet they got vetted before being allowed up though.

"Isn't that overkill?"

Lysander looked at her like he didn't understand what she was asking.

"Is this how you usually travel?" she asked, trying to fathom living like this all of the time. "With a layer of security between you and the rest of the world?"

"Unvetted people are not allowed access to where I am staying, no."

"Doesn't that get exhausting?"

"I don't do the vetting."

"Of course, you don't." She still thought it sounded like it had to be mentally taxing to be so security conscious all the time.

If she really was Mrs. Baros, that would be her life as well. Rowan did her best to ignore the small voice inside her that insisted it would be worth it.

Chapter Twenty-One

Lysander found the couple's massage in the spa surprisingly enjoyable. The ambiance was tranquil in a way the suite could not match regardless of its luxury.

He was glad to see Rowan walking without a single twinge afterward because he had more plans for her in the bedroom later. Or on the balcony...or perhaps they would make use of the sturdy dining table.

However, she looked tired, so he convinced her to return to the suite for a nap. If the sleeping came after he stripped her, spread her legs and tasted the honey between them until she screamed out her climax, he certainly wasn't complaining.

The massage was not the last of Rowan's attempts to draw him into life onboard the cruise ship. Not that she tried to convince him to join her. It was simply that she refused to stay in the suite, and he wasn't about to leave her on her own with a ship full of men looking for a vacation romance, a one-night stand, or both.

Rowan was warm and engaging with everyone they talked to, her beautiful smile on display constantly, her gorgeous body drawing attention wherever they went. Not that his irresistible lover noticed the lascivious stares of other men.

The only thing that kept Lysander from getting homicidal was how totally focused on him she remained.

Right now, they were in the buffet dining room. Not that they were eating here. He drew the line at communal eating from self-serve cafeteria style lines. No matter how high the star rating was for the food here.

It was late in the afternoon on their second day at sea and the large dining area was practically empty.

So, despite having a perfectly adequate study in which to work, Lysander's laptop was on the table in front of him while Rowan read on her tablet in a chair beside the window. She could have read on their balcony, but she wanted to *enjoy the view from this deck,* or so she said.

How much view she was enjoying with her eyes fixed on her eReader was up for interpretation.

An Asian family played Mahjong behind them, the click-clack of tiles interspersed with talking and the occasional sound of victory or groan of defeat.

A few tables away a woman worked on some kind of art project with little gems she painstakingly placed on the picture in front of her. She told every passersby and server who came within six feet of her table about it. Each one heard about how she planned to leave it there for them to finish at the end of the cruise, like she was doing them a favor.

She hadn't tried to talk to him, or Rowan. No doubt because of Klaus and the other three security specialists surrounding them.

Lysander wasn't distracted. He was too focused for that, but he was aware. He noticed everything because that kept him on top and moving forward.

Which was why it really pissed him off that he hadn't realized his father had been wooing a partner investor for his company. He'd discovered that reading a report from his corporate investigator this morning.

Lysander hadn't talked to Rowan about it yet, but he now understood why getting access to her stocks and the piece of real estate was so important to his father and half-brother.

A deal worth hundreds of millions of dollars was at stake.

"Seriously?" Rowan harrumphed.

Lysander looked at her over the top of his computer. Her gaze was on the woman doing the craft project.

"What is it, *glikia mou?*"

"That woman," Rowan hissed and shook her head. "She keeps talking about leaving her gem painting here for the staff to finish, like they have all the time in the world. Like they're on vacation just because she is."

"Why does this bother you?"

"I don't know." She blew out an annoyed breath. "It's just, she's so clueless. No fewer than three servers have tried to politely tell her they don't have time for stuff like that and she keeps overriding them like she knows their workday better than they do."

"And this annoys you?" Lysander asked.

"Yes."

"Why?"

Rowan sighed and looked off into the distance, like she was asking herself that same question.

"It reminds me of traveling with the Andinos," she said after a minute of silent reflection. "They're always so dismissive of anyone paid to serve them in any way."

"She thinks she's doing something nice."

"Right. I know. That makes it worse." Rowan's blue gaze met his, her lovely mouth turned down in a frown.

"Because she wants to be kind?"

"Because she's proud of herself for being *kind* when in fact she's being extremely rude."

Lysander shrugged. "The world is full of oblivious people."

"You're right. And she's not being rude on purpose. Not like my ex and his family, who think they are above anyone not as wealthy as they are."

"They treated you like you were less than because your father's company is not as big."

"I had no voice in that household and I only realized how bad it was after I left, when suddenly I got to make all the choices about my life and how I spent each day." She put her tablet down in her lap and stared out at the ocean again. "My father used me as a bargaining chip to leverage better deals with a company out of his league beforehand."

Was Richard Johnson part of the land development? Rowan was right that her father wasn't a big enough player to be involved in the investment partnership. He would have to have his investigator do some more digging. Knowledge was power.

And Lysander always acted from a position of power.

"Are you ready to return to our suite?" he asked.

Rowan gave him a once over that had his cock hardening. "That depends? Are you done working?"

"I can be."

"Then yes."

~ ~ ~

Their first port of call was Cabo San Lucas.

Rowan had picked an adventure on camelback for their excursion, and she loved it. The guide was voluble and full of anecdotes about the area and its history.

At one point, Lysander made it clear he thought she was paying too much attention to the handsome young man.

Rowan shook her head and laughed at her tycoon. "I'm supposed to hang on his every word. He's telling us about the area."

"And his family. And his own studies at university."

"Which is exactly what makes him so interesting. He's sharing more than what I could read in a guidebook. Thank you so much for finding someone like him to be our guide."

Lysander defrosted enough after that to ask a couple of his own questions.

Afterward, they stopped for lunch at a restaurant in the courtyard of a beautiful building in downtown Cabo San Lucas. Rowan found the outdoor seating charming and spent time people watching while Lysander checked his messages and email on his phone.

Their security detail used a table on either side of them, but there were plenty of other tourists and locals for Rowan to observe. Careful not to get caught staring, she soaked in vignettes of human interaction around her.

But when the fried cheese appetizer arrived, Rowan's attention went to her empty tummy and the delicious food.

"I've never had anything like this," she said.

Lysander hummed an assent, his attention fixed firmly on his phone as he typed away on the screen.

She warned, "If you don't watch out, I'll eat it all."

She'd been expecting something like cheese sticks, but this was cheese flattened and fried, to be eaten like chips with the plethora of salsas in little dishes on the table.

"I'll wait for my lunch," Lysander said without looking up.

At the reminder that more food was coming, Rowan had one last bite of the cheese and then pushed the platter away.

Taking a sip of her fresh coconut water, Rowan noticed a familiar woman walking purposefully between the tables.

Adele Fournier stopped beside their table. "Lysander, darling, if you are that bored with your companion, perhaps you should have answered my latest text."

Lysander's head jerked up. "Adele."

His expression was filled with surprise and in no way welcoming. Rowan was gobsmacked. What was the supermodel doing here? Was she on a shoot? What were the odds?

"You don't mind if I join you?" Adele asked, finally deigning to acknowledge Rowan with a lift of her perfectly shaped eyebrows.

Neither Rowan, nor Lysander had a chance to reply before the model sat down in one of the empty chairs at their table.

Rowan opened her mouth to say she did in fact mind, but didn't get a chance.

Klaus was already there physically lifting Adele from the chair. "This is a private lunch, Miz Fournier. Let me help you find another table."

"What? Klaus, release me at once. Lys, tell this behemoth to take his hands off me."

"I prefer *goon*," Klaus said in an aside to Rowan, inexorably guiding the still complaining supermodel away from the table.

"Why bother inviting me to Mexico if you're going to treat me like this?" she shouted at Lysander over her shoulder as she struggled against Klaus's grip. "I won't stand for it."

Lysander ignored the mini temper tantrum happening behind him and snagged Rowan's gaze with his own. "I did not invite her. I don't know what she's doing here."

"How did she know you were here though?" Rowan asked. "I thought no one was supposed to know where we are."

"That is something Klaus is no doubt attempting to find out."

Klaus, who apparently preferred Rowan's teasing moniker of goon over behemoth, was speaking quietly to Adele as he marched her out of the restaurant.

"Did she let you know she planned to be here too?" This all felt a bit surreal.

How was Adele Fournier, of all people, in Cabo San Lucas the same day they were?

"If she did, I don't know about it. I deleted her contact info from the text app we used to communicate." Nothing about Lysander's demeanor said he had wanted to see the other woman, much less done as she claimed and invited her to join him in Mexico.

"She doesn't have your number?"

"No."

"I do."

"Yes."

Rowan sighed. "One word answers? Really?"

"What would you like me to say?"

"I'm not sure. You were dating her last year."

"You know that is not true. I explained it to you. She was my plus one at a few events. We were not dating."

"You never answered when I asked if you have sex with her." It had been implied, but not spelled out.

Suddenly, Rowan needed things to be crystal clear in her mind.

"Does it matter?"

"Yes." She could do one-word answers too.

Lysander looked amused rather than worried. "Jealous? You were married to Cyrus for most of the time Adele acted as my plus one."

Rowan pretended not to hear the question about her jealousy, not sure if that was what she was feeling, or not. She'd never been jealous before. Not even when she'd discovered her husband had a mistress and a string of extra-marital lovers.

Angry and betrayed? Yes. Jealous? No.

"Did you?" she pressed.

"Once."

"Oh." Although Rowan had no doubt that Adele wanted to be in Lysander's bed, the feeling had not been mutual.

"Before I learned she'd been with Cyrus."

Okay, so maybe not so much he hadn't wanted the supermodel, but Lysander didn't want his brother's ex. Only that didn't make any sense, because he definitely wanted Rowan. He showed her several times a day.

"Oh." Rowan cringed inwardly at how inarticulate she sounded.

"I don't talk about women after I've had sex with them, but the fact it only happened one time and she was my companion on multiple occasions should tell you something."

It wasn't about Adele being one of Cyrus's exes. Lysander was clearly implying that the sex hadn't been great. Simply put, Lysander hadn't been that into the supermodel.

That's what the admission told her. Also, Lysander was a gentleman, if a ruthless one, because he didn't say anything overtly disparaging about Adele. Which he could have done to make his case seem more believable.

But the Greek billionaire didn't think he needed to make a case. He expected Rowan to believe him. Which she did.

Relief washed over Rowan, though really...it should not matter. But it really did.

"She calls you Lys."

"Which I have instructed her multiple times not to do. It is one of the reasons I stopped having my assistant set her up as my plus one."

"Your assistant set it up?"

"Yes."

"Huh."

"I would never have personally invited her to Mexico if I wanted her here to attend a function with me. I would have left it up to my staff to arrange."

Did he think Rowan had doubts? She didn't. "I believe you," she spelled out, in case he needed her to.

He nodded, like he expected no less, but the tension around his eyes lessened. "Before you, I didn't do relationships that mattered. Hell, I didn't do real relationships at all. I had sexual liaisons that lasted months without a single personal discussion between us."

Not like them. Rowan and Lysander talked about everything from their favorite music, food, and entertainment to family and their hopes for the future.

"What we have, it's real." It wasn't a question. Rowan knew it was.

Whether it was temporary, or not, what they shared went deeper than convenience, or even sexual hunger.

"It is."

The rest of their lunch went uninterrupted. When Klaus returned from seeing the supermodel on her way, he did not sit back down, but remained standing on alert until they were ready to leave.

No other uninvited guests would be sitting at their table.

CHAPTER TWENTY-TWO

On their fourth day aboard ship, Rowan finally convinced Lysander to have dinner in one of the specialty restaurants.

Their security team filled the tables around them, but Rowan didn't let that bother her. Soaking in the over-the-top luxury décor, including a chandelier the size of her car, she observed the other diners and the waitstaff interact.

"You like to watch people," Lysander remarked.

"I always have. I'm an extroverted-introvert. I'll chat with people, but I'm just as happy to watch them from the background."

"You are hardly in the background here."

No. He'd made sure they had a very nice table with a view of the ocean. Other passengers kept sending them looks. She supposed with their entourage of bodyguards, they looked famous, or something. People probably wondered who they were.

"We are a little conspicuous in how our group takes up five tables." Two security personnel sat at each of four around them. And then of course there was their table.

"Klaus and the others could be eating in the privacy of their suite if we were eating in ours," Lysander pointed out, not so helpfully.

Rowan gave her lover a look. "Maybe they would have eaten here anyway."

"I'm sure they would not."

"Let's ask them." Which is what she did, proving her point.

Every single one of the security personnel said they preferred eating out in such a controlled environment.

Huh.

That wasn't something Rowan had considered, how guarding Lysander aboard ship, even when he was out of the suite, was easier than back in Athens.

"Don't get smug," Lysander told her, but his eyes were smiling, even if his lips weren't.

Dinner was delicious and even he had to admit it. Which she made him do before she would leave the table.

"You are a challenge." He shook his head. "Why do I put up with you?"

"Because you like my body?"

"I like more than your body. And I adore your body, let's be clear on that."

"Hmm, I think I like being in the adored category."

"You are the only one that ever has been."

This man.

When he said things like that, Rowan had a hard time remembering he didn't want long term commitment. Only maybe he'd changed his attitude about that just like she had?

It was such a tantalizing thought that Rowan had to banish it very firmly. If she let herself hope for a future with Lysander and he decided he was done with her a month from now, her heart would break.

She'd never had a broken heart before, but she'd known plenty of emotional pain with her family and her ex. She suspected Lysander had the power to devastate her in a way no one else had.

~ ~ ~

Their next day at anchor was in Puerto Vallarta where she'd chosen a private tequila tasting, followed by a fiesta lunch with traditional dancers and a discussion of their history in the area.

Although Rowan was not a big drinker, she easily discerned the vast difference between aged tequila and what she'd had in margaritas when she'd gone for a drink with coworkers after work.

She listened avidly to the lecture on the process of harvesting the agave and distilling the tequila.

She even got to meet a *jimadore*, one of the skilled workers who harvested the agave. They chatted for nearly half an hour, and he proudly told her about the long line of men in his family who had been *jimadores*.

After lunch, they visited the cathedral, which was awe inspiring and had such an air of peace, she'd put off leaving as long as possible.

That peace was shattered when they stepped outside.

"Lysander, fancy seeing you here." It was Cyrus.

"You have a serious security breach," Rowan said to Lysander. "First your ex and now mine."

"What the hell are you doing here?" Lysander demanded of his half-brother.

"Taking in the sites like you, I would imagine."

"Cut the crap, Cyrus. I don't know how you tracked us down, but your intrusion is not welcome."

"Oh, was this little trip to Mexico supposed to be a secret?" Cyrus asked. "I'm sure I saw some speculation about it with a picture of you two."

Lysander said a very ugly word. Rowan didn't chastise him. She was feeling the same way.

Until the threats to him were dealt with, Lysander was at risk. She hated knowing someone had revealed their whereabouts. Could it have been Ariston Spiridakou? But why would he?

Lysander did not bother replying to Cyrus, but ushered Rowan into one of the shops on a side street near the cathedral. His security team prevented Cyrus from following them or speaking to them.

Unless he wanted to shout and that was below her ex-husband's self-perceived dignity.

Rowan didn't want to let Cyrus showing up spoil the day, but tension made her shoulders tight as she and Lysander perused the shops. He even helped her find tchotchkes to give her coworkers back in Athens. Which she found endearing.

However, she didn't relax again until she and Lysander were strolling along the sea walk, marveling at the view of the harbor and her annoying ex was nowhere in sight.

"There is someplace I would like to go, if you're up for one more stop?" Lysander asked. "I know Cyrus showing up put a pall on the day."

Rowan shook her head vehemently. "No. It has been an amazing day and I've really enjoyed how you've indulged my inner tourist."

"Then you don't mind one last stop?"

"Not at all." Since Rowan hadn't had anything else on her itinerary, she had no idea where Lysander wanted to take her. "What did you want to see?"

"It's a surprise."

The surprise turned out to be a jewelry store with a team of jewelers on hand who either worked on new pieces or made adjustments to jewelry bought on site. They did all of this at their workbenches in full view of the store.

Rowan was fascinated.

"Here, try this on," Lysander said from beside her.

A large pendant with a gorgeous teardrop shaped Mexican fire opal and a cluster of diamonds at the top dangled from a gold chain in his hand.

He'd been over on the other side of the store, and she'd assumed he was checking his phone again. Apparently, he'd been perusing the jewelry cases.

"It's beautiful," Rowan breathed.

"An opal that size is very rare, but especially a fire opal," the jeweler who she'd been watching fashion a one of a kind ring said.

"It reminds me of your hair," Lysander said as he fixed the chain around her neck.

The shimmery red stone with streaks of opalescence settled just above her cleavage.

Brandishing a mirror, the salesclerk said, "Ah, it is almost as lovely as the woman wearing it."

Rowan looked at her image in the mirror and something tugged at her heart. Not because of the necklace, but because of the expression on Lysander's face beside hers.

There was more fire in his eyes than in the opal.

"It suits you, *yineka mou*."

For some reason, Rowan's throat was too tight to make speech so she nodded. She loved it.

"There it is finished." The jeweler held up the ring he'd been working on. "You must try it on."

The ring was a delicate brushed gold band that came together in two hearts entwined around a much smaller fire opal than the one in her pendant.

Rowan was going to refuse when Lysander took the ring. Grabbing her hand, he lifted it so he could slide the golden circle onto her left ring finger.

In Greece that ring finger had no particular significance, as wedding rings were worn on the right hand, but in America, it symbolized promises and engagements.

"Perfect," Lysander said.

Rowan's gaze snapped up to his, but he was looking at the ring on her finger.

"Such a special woman deserves this special ring," the jeweler said.

It was then the haggling began. Lysander might be a billionaire, but he was also Greek. After several minutes of a spirited back and forth, Rowan walked out of the store wearing both the pendant and the ring.

"There you are," a feminine voice filled with satisfaction said when they walked out of the shop.

Klaus and the other guards immediately surrounded Rowan and Lysander, preventing Adele from getting close.

She gave them a moue of displeasure. "Really, this is too much. You all know me. I am no threat to Lys. I am a world renowned model."

She was a world class pain in the backside. However, she'd found them the first time, learning their itinerary once she knew what ship they were sailing on wouldn't have been hard. What Rowan couldn't figure out was why she was here in the Mexico to begin with.

Finding it difficult to believe that such a famous woman would be stalking Lysander, Rowan's mind chewed over the possibilities.

Was she here on her own? Or had someone put her up to it? Rowan knew who she suspected for the latter. Cyrus or Baptiste Andino. Cyrus being at the top of her list because he too had shown up today.

But honestly? What could her ex-husband hope to gain?

"Whoever put you up to this won't be able to protect you if I decide to torpedo your career," Lysander said to Adele, echoing Rowan's suspicion that the supermodel was not in Mexico on her own agenda.

Fear flashed in the model's eyes, but then she smiled and gave Lysander a flirty look. "Don't pretend you don't know why I'm here."

"Leave, Adele, now. And I won't make a call to your agency. Don't leave and you won't be able find work in an online clothing catalogue."

Tears welled into the other woman's eyes and she looked at Lysander reproachfully. "Stop threatening me. I haven't done anything wrong."

"Now." That was all Lysander said.

But Adele spun on her heel and walked away.

"Follow her," Lysander said to Klaus. "I want to know if she meets up with Cyrus."

So, he suspected collusion between their exes as well.

Whatever was driving her, they didn't see Adele Fournier again.

CHAPTER TWENTY-THREE

Rowan woke early to an empty bed. Again.

She forced herself to get up and throw a cotton sundress on. After running her fingers through her hair to try to tame it, she left the bedroom, determined to join Lysander for breakfast.

He had been working longer hours since Puerto Vallarta and she'd barely seen him the last couple of days. He'd been so busy, he didn't even bother to complain, much less offer to join her, when she left their suite to experience all she could of shipboard life.

They ate dinner together, but even then, he spent more time on his phone than talking to her.

She couldn't help wondering if he was growing bored with her, or maybe Cyrus's shenanigans were getting to be too much for Lysander, Mr. No Drama Here Folks, to deal with.

He hadn't come to bed until almost three in the morning last night and they hadn't made love. He'd slept only a few hours before getting up again.

Would this be their new norm when they returned to Athens? And if it was, how was she going to handle it? They'd spent more time together before the cruise than they did now, on their so called vacation.

A vacation necessitated by security, but still.

How long before he asked her to move back into her apartment? Or before she decided to go to save herself the grief of rejection?

Today, she was inserting herself into his day, if only for breakfast. Rowan found him on the balcony, looking at his phone. Of course.

There was a cup of coffee on the table, but no food.

"Good morning. Have you had breakfast?" she asked.

Lysander looked up from the small screen, satisfaction covering his handsome features. "We've got them."

"Who them?" Then she realized. "The people threatening you? They've been arrested?"

"Better." His dark gaze burned with purpose. "I dismantled the business. The men in power are now scrambling to keep their homes and cars as their company implodes. Newsflash: they won't."

"You're going to bankrupt them personally?" she asked. Wouldn't that make the men's hatred for him more personal too?

"It is already happening."

"But won't that make them want to kill you even more?"

"They won't have enough money to buy toys for their children's birthdays much less hire muscle to come after me."

"That's awful. Children should not suffer for their parents' bad judgment."

"You would prefer I left these men with the resources to remain a threat to me? To you?" The way he said *to you* told Rowan that she was one of the main reasons he was being so thorough in dismantling the business empire and the lives of the men who ran it.

Which meant what? He *wasn't* bored with her? She cautioned herself not to read too much into it. Apparently, he'd been protective of her before they'd ever shared a bed.

"No," she denied quickly. The thought of something happening to Lysander made her sick. "But can't you make sure their children don't end up on the streets?"

Even as she asked the question, she realized how foolish she sounded.

Lysander didn't look at her with judgment or pity for her naivete though. His gaze burned, but no longer with the zeal of revenge. Something else entirely smoldered in those brown orbs now. Something she was afraid to name.

"Come here," he said.

With zero instinct to protest, Rowan obeyed and as soon as she reached him, Lysander pulled her into his lap. Cupping her face, he kissed her. She wrapped her arms around his neck and kissed him back.

Things were heating up nicely when he broke the kiss. She made a sound of protest.

But he pulled back until their gazes met. "You are something special."

"I don't think so."

"I know so." He kissed her forehead and then her lips again, but chastely this time. "For you, *glikia mou*, I will arrange something for the wives and children."

It took several seconds for Rowan's scattered senses to understand what he was referring to. Protecting the children.

Worry that doing so would leave him vulnerable instantly filled her heart. "It will have to be resources those men can't leverage. They can't be left with any way to hurt you."

"Do not worry. When I take an enemy down, they stay down."

She shivered, but it wasn't with fear. It was with arousal. His power and confidence were a total turn on for her.

"You like that."

She shrugged. "Maybe. A little. You're like a tycoon superhero."

The kiss he gave her sent all of Rowan's concerns for the future into the ether, right along with her ability to string two thoughts together.

They spent the entire day at sea together, but never once left the suite and rarely left the bedroom, unless it was to spend naked time together in the hot tub.

~ ~ ~

When the ship arrived in Ensenada and they disembarked, Rowan was not surprised a private car waited to take them to the Kumiai Reservation. And she was relieved to see no sign of either Adele or Cyrus.

She was stunned, however, when they were joined by a group of tourists from the ship after they got there. Lysander had not booked a private experience.

It was because she'd said she wished they could be regular tourists, just once. It had been a throw away comment when she was drowsy after lovemaking.

Despite his clear desire to give her what she'd said she wanted, Lysander's security team created a wall between them and the other guests while they listened to a fascinating lecture on the history and traditional ways of the Kumiai people in the museum.

Well, she listened. He took a call outside. He returned only after they had been ushered to a long dining table and everyone else had been given samplings of food that would have been staples of the Kumiai people's diet in the past.

He frowned when he reached the table to find all the seats around Rowan taken. And not by his security. She'd told the men to stand back unless they planned to participate. Nothing was going to happen to her with them looming against the wall less than six feet away.

Rowan sat across from an older couple who acted like they were on their honeymoon, only to tell her they'd been married for decades. They were near the end of the table where a man from the ship who was supposed to rate the tour for their cruise director was seated.

He was friendly, but not as outgoing as the man to her left, who seemed intent on learning everything that there was to know about her. Rowan evaded answering his probing personal questions, wondering if he was some kind of paparazzi on Lysander's scent.

"So, you're single?" he asked, his gaze well south of her eyes.

Not a reporter. A guy on the make.

Rowan wasn't interested and she opened her mouth to say so, but Lysander's hand landed heavily on her shoulder, surprising her into silence.

"No. She is not," he gritted out.

Oh, somebody's phone call hadn't gone well.

"Is this a shipboard thing, or something more?" the man asked.

Wow. That was so bold, and deluded, Rowan had to stifle a laugh.

"None of your business. There's an empty seat further up the table. Take it." Lysander's voice was deep with unspoken menace.

Without another word, the overly friendly man vacated his chair.

Lysander sat down and then took Rowan's hand in his. He didn't try any of the food, but he paid attention when the guides spoke. He even turned his phone to silent.

Afterward, they learned how to make a woven pendant for a necklace. Rowan's reeds broke almost immediately, and the teacher had to weave extra fibers onto it so she could continue. Naturally, Lysander's turned out perfectly. And he finished first.

"Show off," Rowan muttered as she worked on finishing hers off.

He cocked an eyebrow. "Do you want me to help you?"

"No."

But he got up to lean over her anyway and his hands came around hers, guiding her fingers in twisting the wet reeds. Rowan's breath sped up and her body reacted predictably to his touch and nearness.

She was just grateful no one else seemed to notice.

Until the woman who'd sat across from her during the food demonstration said, "What a sweetheart." And her husband gave Lysander a knowing look. "Yep. Sweet. That's the word."

He knew exactly what her Greek billionaire was doing to her, and his expression said he approved. With the way he cuddled his wife during the lecture from the elders, he no doubt did.

There. She got it.

Needing a break from Lysander's nearness before she combusted or begged him to take a walk behind the buildings with her, Rowan joined in the traditional dance. She was out of step as often as not, but she had fun.

It didn't give her the reprieve she'd needed though because her tycoon watched her with burning eyes.

She was more than a little grateful for the private car on their trip back into the city. As soon as he closed the privacy panel between the back and the front, Lysander made good on the promise of those heated looks.

Chapter Twenty-Four

They stopped at the city center on the way back to the ship and did some shopping.

"These are all tourist shops along this road. Are you sure this is where you want to shop?" Lysander asked her for the third time as they entered a store filled with t-shirts.

"Yes." Rowan perused the t-shirts and chatted with the salesperson in Spanish.

Her Spanish was rusty as she had little chance to use it in her life in Athens, but the salesclerk didn't seem to mind. She told Rowan about her family, including her younger sister who was attending college.

Rowan insisted on getting matching t-shirts for herself and Lysander.

"I will never wear it," he warned.

"Didn't anyone ever tell you to never say never?"

"No."

She smiled and shook her head. "We'll see."

She picked out t-shirts for Iona and her husband as well.

"Who are those for?" Lysander asked.

"Your mom and her husband."

"You think my mother will wear a souvenir t-shirt?"

Rowan shrugged. "Probably to paint in."

Lysander's mother was an artist. Her paintings were swaths of color and no discernable shapes, but they made her happy. And Rowan really liked the few that Lysander had hanging on his walls.

They always evoked emotion.

"And where do you think her husband will wear his?"

"He probably won't, but it would be rude to get her one and not him."

Lysander just shook his head, but his lips tilted in an almost smile that turned into a full on grin when he said, "Perhaps we should get one for my father."

Rowan laughed, but Lysander went on the hunt for the tackiest possible t-shirt with the loudest colors to buy for Baptiste. She didn't suggest getting anything for Baptiste's latest wife, not even as a joke.

Rowan was sure the woman would never be anything but a sore spot for Lysander.

They visited handbag shops and Rowan bought a roomy beach tote that would bring back memories of this trip when she used it.

Her feet were sore by the time they returned to the ship and Lysander suggested she soak in the hot tub while he got some work done. "I would like to join you, but dismantling a company takes time. Things that were not critical are now because of the timing."

Oh. That made sense of the days he'd worked pretty much nonstop. They weren't a harbinger for the future, except when he had a big deal going. And Rowan could live with that, so long as it was the exception and not the norm.

Besides, when he was done, he'd taken a full day off to be with her. *In bed*, that little voice of caution in her head reminded her.

While their relationship was more than sex, at her insistence, it existed because of their explosive sexual attraction. Letting herself forget that would set her up for heartache.

Unwilling to dwell on those thoughts, even if she also refused to ignore them, Rowan changed into her bikini.

She came out onto the balcony to find a bowl of frozen grapes and a carafe of chilled water (with ice, which was her preference and an American habit she'd never let go of) on the hot tub ledge.

Lysander.

She gave a swoony sigh she never would have let anyone else hear.

He could be so incredibly thoughtful.

When her body was fully relaxed from soaking in the bubbling water, and she felt refreshed from the frozen grapes and crisp, cool water, Rowan got out. Taking the remainder of the carafe of water with her, she settled on a lounger. The sun felt so good on her body, she just lazed while her thoughts drifted and she watched the people come and go on the deck two stories below.

She should have brought her tablet out to read, but couldn't make herself get up and retrieve it.

"You have forgotten to frost the glass again," Lysander said as he pressed the button.

"I didn't forget." In fact, she'd had to turn it back to clear.

Given his way, Lysander would have left it frosted twenty-four-seven.

"And yet here you lie with your luscious body on display."

"Thank you."

"For what?"

"Calling my body luscious." She smiled up at him. "You make me feel beautiful."

"You are beautiful, and I do not want my goddess of a lover the subject of other men's fantasies."

Rowan laughed. She could not help it. "You are always so complimentary." But she was no goddess. "The only way anyone can see me up here is if they have better than normal vision, or binoculars and who is going to go to that effort?"

The sun loungers were set toward the back of the balcony as well. The angle would make spying on her even more difficult than the distance. If anyone were that keen to do so.

"You refuse to see yourself as the irresistible woman that you are."

"As long as you can't resist me, that's all that I care about."

"I cannot. Why do you think I am out here when I still have a dozen unopened emails marked urgent in my in-box?"

Warmth curled through her all the way down to her toes. "Am I keeping you from your work?" she teased.

He growled and started stripping off his clothes.

~ ~ ~

It was more difficult than Rowan expected to return to normal life in Athens. Well, her new normal, living with her sexually irresistible billionaire lover.

Living with Lysander wasn't the hard part and hadn't been since the day she moved in. Getting used to his demanding work schedule was. He'd always worked longer hours than her, but since they got back from Mexico, he worked less from his office in the villa.

There were days the only time she saw him was when he woke her in the middle of the night to make love.

With one exception, the evenings he made it home for dinner, his attention was entirely on Rowan however. That exception had been when they had dinner with his mother and her husband. The older couple had been charmed by the kitchy t-shirts, though Iona's husband had clearly been more impressed with the aged tequila Lysander gifted him.

Most nights they ate alone at the villa. However, sometimes Lysander took her to A List restaurants, where he always arranged for some sort of private dining for them, so they could eat undisturbed.

Being the center of his intense focus was becoming as addictive as his lovemaking, but on the days she didn't see him at all, Rowan spent way too much time thinking.

Before their trip to Mexico, they texted back and forth throughout the day. Since returning to Athens, he often took an hour, or longer, to reply to her texts. There were times when she hadn't asked a specific question that he did not reply at all. And, unlike before their trip, he rarely initiated a text conversation.

Their first week back, she'd chalked that up to him being busy catching up with work. By the second week, the pang she got when her texts went unanswered felt more like a knife jab to her tender heart.

She'd been so sure she could keep deep emotions out of this thing between them.

Boy, had she been wrong about that.

Rowan's heart was fully engaged while she suspected Lysander's was still firmly locked behind the protective barriers he'd never let down.

The fear that he was growing bored with her that she'd managed to banish aboard ship came rushing back. She'd convinced herself that his distant behavior had been due to how busy he'd been de-toothing the bite of his enemies.

Now, she questioned that belief.

Because there were no more enemies to crush into corporate dust and he was just as distant, if not more so. At least he hadn't told her about any further threats. She only had one bodyguard assigned to her now though. Which supported her belief that it was back to life as usual for her tycoon.

Was he hers though? While he still called her *glikia mou*, his sweet, he hadn't used the more intimate and meaningful term *yineka mou*, his woman, since their return to Athens. Not even during sex.

Deciding she needed a break from her disquieting thoughts, Rowan accepted her coworker's invitation to get drinks after work.

"I believe Mr. Baros plans to be home this evening," Klaus told Rowan when she informed him of her plans.

So, he had time to text his security, but not her? "If he expected me to be there as well, I'm sure he would have let me know."

Ignoring Klaus's frown, Rowan joined her coworkers on the walk to the bar. Drinks turned into dinner, and she didn't get back to the villa until after nine.

She found Lysander in his inner sanctum, a laptop on his lap and the television playing international news in the background.

"You have a real problem relaxing, don't you?" she asked with a shake of her head as she dropped her oversized purse on the floor near one end of the sectional.

Lysander glared at her hold-all like it offended him. "Are you going to leave that there?"

"Until I need it again tomorrow morning, yes. Why? Is there somewhere else you'd rather I put it?"

"Your closet." His tone implied she should realize that was the appropriate place to store her bag.

Her pleasant buzz from her evening was disappearing like the mist. "Okay," she said drawing out both syllables. "If it bothered you, you could have said something before."

"I'm saying something now."

"Noted." She picked up the bag and headed out of the room to stow it upstairs in her closet.

"Where are you going?" he asked, sounding surly.

"To put my purse away, like you so pleasantly told me to."

"Petulance doesn't become you."

"I'm not being petulant. I *was* being sarcastic because you have *not* been pleasant, but I am also adult enough to respect your wish for me not to clutter your home with my things. Now, if you will excuse me."

"It is your home too." Take surly and add it to supremely irritated and throw in a dash of righteous indignation and that was Lysander's tone now.

Her patience about used up, Rowan gritted her teeth and nodded. Because right now? This didn't feel like her home so much as somewhere she was staying on sufferance.

"Put it away later. I haven't seen you all day."

"It's hardly the first time this week." It was in fact, the first time he'd gotten back to the villa before she went to bed since the weekend. "I'm going to take a shower and then go to bed."

"Is that an invitation?" He stood, his masculine presence dominating and intense.

Her lady parts immediately pulsed with heat and wetness flooded her panties.

Refusing to show how easily he got to her, she forced a casual shrug. "You're welcome to join me. You can work on your laptop while I read."

There. He could put that in his pipe and smoke it.

She dropped her hold-all on the floor of her side of the massive walk-in closet before kicking off her shoes and stowing them with her others. Passing Lysander on her way through the bedroom, she did her best to ignore his brooding presence. Which was a total failure as every nerve ending in her body sparked from his nearness.

Rowan stripped and tossed her clothes in the hamper before stepping into the oversized marble shower. Turning on the water, she jumped as cold water showered down before the hot water followed. It was only a second or two, but it woke her up.

"No need to punish yourself with a cold shower," Lysander drawled as he stepped in behind her.

"I'm not," she groused. "I've done nothing that needs punishing."

"You know I work long hours. I expect you to be here when I am."

Heck to the no. "If you want my company, you can *ask* for it."

"I told Klaus I would be home tonight. Are you saying he didn't inform you?"

"No." Rowan put her head back under the cascading water and closed her eyes.

"So, why didn't you come home?"

"Because I was invited by my friends to join them for drinks."

"You could have gone for drinks with them any other night."

Lathering her hair, she opened her eyes to glare at her arrogant lover. "And you could have texted me instead of Klaus if you wanted my company."

Even if Lysander had texted *her*, Rowan would like to think that it was not a given she would have blown off her plans with her coworkers. Not in the habit of lying to herself, she acknowledged she probably would have. She missed spending time with her lover.

"Do not be childish. You knew I was going to be here."

That was the second time he'd implied she was behaving immaturely, and man did it prick her temper. "There is nothing puerile about expecting common courtesy."

His dark gaze traveled over her body, leaving heated sensation in its wake. "No, there is nothing childlike about you. I should have said obstinate."

"You think I'm being stubborn?" she asked, her own gaze narrowed even as her vaginal walls contracted with the need to have him inside her.

Ignoring her body's cravings, she rinsed her hair and waited for his answer.

It came in the form of his hands cupping her breasts. "Yes, I think you were foolishly stubborn to spend the evening with your friends when you could have been here, doing this with me."

Chapter Twenty-Five

"Sex isn't everything." And they'd agreed it wouldn't be the only thing between them either.

"But it is something good," he said. "Something special."

Rowan wasn't feeling all that special, no matter how intensely her body reacted to his touch. Not with him expecting her to abandon her plans at the last minute because he was going to be unexpectedly available.

Even worse if it wasn't unexpected. If he'd known from the beginning of their day that he would be back at the villa in time for dinner.

Unaware of her tumultuous thoughts, Lysander took the conditioner bottle from her hand. "Let me."

He squirted a fair amount in his hand and then worked it through her hair, massaging her scalp until she relaxed against him. Then, showing he remembered her routine, he began to wash her body with soapy hands.

As she might expect, her lover paid particular attention to her breasts and between her legs, but he also knelt so he could thoroughly clean each of her feet, rubbing his fingers between her toes.

Pleasure zinged straight from her feet to her core. Shocked at how good that felt, she gasped.

"You like that, *yineka mou?*"

The physical sensation mixed with his use of that endearment made Rowan's knees buckle. He caught her. Of course. Rising, he snaked one arm around her waist and used his other hand to help rinse the conditioner from her hair.

When he was done, he turned off the water and moved them from the shower. He dried her off before handing her a fresh towel to wrap her hair in, turban style. He took a lot less time drying his own body than he had hers.

"I have to dry my hair." She hated going to sleep with wet hair. Not only did it look like an awful mess in the morning, but it soaked her pillow.

"Sit down. I'll do it."

"Are you trying to make up for being so grumpy when I got home?" She sat on the stool in front of the built in vanity.

"Maybe I just enjoy spoiling you." He carefully pulled the towel from her head and then used it to wick more moisture away from her hair.

Afterward, he gently brushed her hair and then used her blow dryer to finish drying it.

"You're awfully good at this." Was it something he'd done for all of his lovers? Only it was the first time he'd dried *her* hair.

"I watched you and I am a fast learner."

"Are you saying you don't make it a habit to dry your girlfriend's hair?" she pressed, unsure why it felt so important to know.

"You are the only woman I have done this for." His lips turned down in a frown and his jaw hardened.

"You don't have to do it. I can finish."

His head and shoulders moved like he was shaking off his thoughts. "No."

Okay, then.

He finished and ran his fingers through her long red hair, smoothed by his near professional attention to it. "It is so silky."

"That's what the conditioner is for," she quipped.

Leaning down, he slid his hands over her breasts and cupped them. "I think it is you. Everything about you is soft to my touch. Your hair is silk, your skin smooth like satin."

Heat bloomed in her cheeks. "You're awfully complimentary."

He didn't answer, but his big hands gently kneaded her fleshy curves. Mesmerized, she watched him watch her in the mirror as her nipples beaded and the flush of arousal washed over her chest and up her neck.

His own dark gaze flared with arousal.

"These luscious, pink buds are irresistible." Lysander plucked at her nipples, sending sensation thrumming through Rowan.

More wet heat gathered between her legs, and she squirmed, that feeling of emptiness in her core growing.

"You respond so beautifully to my touch, *yineka mou*." He leaned down and kissed her neck, his tongue tasting her clean skin. "It makes me very happy."

Warmth unfurled inside of her and her annoyance at his grumpiness melted under the heat of their combined arousal. The scent and heat of his body surrounded her as he straightened, once again meeting her gaze in the mirror. The storm raging through her reflected in the depth of his eyes.

Rowan turned her head so she could rub her cheek against the join of his hip and torso, her hair brushing over his erection. The engorged flesh jumped, and he groaned.

His hands tightened on her swollen mounds, his fingertips pinching her rigid nipples to the point of pain before brushing over them in a soothing caress. "I want you."

"You have me." She turned on the stool and licked a pearl of pre-ejaculate off the tip of his hard penis.

She reveled in the salty sweetness of him before he came, swiping over his slit a second time.

His hands came to rest on her head on both sides, his hold firm but not harsh and he pressed against her parted lips with his erection. "Open."

She did as he ordered, and he pushed the head of his shaft into her willing mouth. She sucked and laved him with her tongue.

They both loved this. Him in her mouth, Lysander controlling their pleasure. Rowan didn't touch his sex with her hands, but let him use her mouth as he liked while she steadied herself with a hold on the rock hard muscles of his thighs.

He pushed a couple of inches of his oversized sex into her mouth. "That's good. Take me."

Rowan sucked, welcoming him as he stretched her mouth wide, pushing toward the back of her throat. He didn't gag her, but pistoned in and out of her as she sucked and licked. She tasted his copious precum as his erection swelled and became even more granite-like.

He was close and her mouth watered with anticipation of his climax, but he pulled out of her mouth with a pop. Saliva covered her chin and glistened on his rigid sex.

Confused by his withdrawal, her gaze flew upward. A look of carnal need hardened his features.

Lysander grabbed her under her arms and jerked her up and kissed her almost brutally before spinning her body around. He positioned her so she faced the mirror, her torso leaning forward on the vanity, balanced on her forearms.

His features cast in vicious desire, he shoved into her dripping channel from behind. She was tight and he was big, so even though she was slick with arousal, shock reverberated through her at the intimate intrusion.

Rowan watched in the mirror as his handsome face reflected the savage ecstasy he found in their connection.

He hammered forward, drilling his big erection deep into her body, stretching her vaginal walls as only he ever had. Lysander hit that spot inside her that brought so much pleasure and she moaned.

"Mine," he growled as he bottomed out against her cervix.

Mild pain mixed with pleasure, intensifying it to near unbearable levels. And she shuddered as her own climax loomed. He pulled back before pounding into her again, repeatedly sliding over her G-spot and battering her cervix with his bulbous head.

When she thought she might pass out from the tension inside her, Rowan finally detonated. Bliss exploded from her core outward, forcing a scream from deep inside her.

He shoved forward, going rigid as his penis pressed against the very depth of her as he gave a guttural shout, their orgasms feeding off each other. He filled her with his heat, making her shudder with renewed pleasure, his grip on her hips so tight it would probably leave bruises.

The idea of having his fingerprints on her skin sent another wave of ecstasy crashing through her before she collapsed forward, boneless in the aftermath of the mind numbing bliss.

She was too wiped afterward to protest when he carried her to bed without showering again. But also...she liked the scent of them together on her skin. She'd bathe in the morning. Maybe.

~ ~ ~

Lysander got into his office before dawn, wishing he could have stayed in bed to make love to Rowan again, but there was too much to do.

He had lost out on not one, but two lucrative deals while playing tourist with Rowan in Mexico. Since starting his company, he had never let the ball drop when there was profit to be made.

Not until taking the maddening woman as his lover.

Why had she insisted on going to dinner with her coworkers when she knew he was at the villa waiting for her? He didn't like this feeling of need she engendered in him. Lysander controlled every aspect of his life and his business until Rowan Johnson had offered him her body.

He'd begun to work shorter hours until making the inexplicable choice to take her on the cruise in Mexico she'd always wanted. When logic would dictate he spend the time out of country at one of his other headquarters.

Lysander hadn't minded the money he lost by not being available to orchestrate the deals. And that had bothered him a hell of a lot more than losing the money. He ran a multi-billion dollar company. He had thousands of employees relying on him keeping that company in the black.

How could one small woman disrupt the discipline of a lifetime?

He'd thrown himself into work since returning to Athens, determined to make up for his slacking, only to leave his office early the day before. Because he'd missed her.

And she had opted to spend the evening with others.

It pissed him off. And it...hurt. Though he would never admit that particular vulnerability.

Her schedule was a lot more flexible than his. She should accommodate him. Why did she not realize that?

~ ~ ~

"Excuse me? You think we're going where?"

Rowan couldn't quite wrap her mind around what Lysander had just said.

"Japan."

"Another time, I would love to travel to Japan with you." Or anywhere else. "But I just got back from a vacation. I cannot take another one. Especially right now."

"I will get one of my employees to cover for you," he said dismissively.

"No. That won't work this time." Like in most nonprofit organizations, employees like her wore many hats.

Rowan had been put in charge of their major fundraising gala. The director believed the connections she'd made during her ill fated marriage could be leveraged to bring in bigger donations than ever before.

She agreed, but needed to reach out personally to donors and sponsors for that to work.

"You were okay with it in order to take the cruise you wanted. Now you refuse so we can spend the next two weeks together."

That was so unfair. Did she want to spend two weeks apart? No. But that did not change the fact that Rowan could not leave Athens right now.

"First, you did not actually give me a choice. Second, we left Greece for safety reasons and the choice to go on a cruise was subordinate to that. Third, I am up to my ears in planning the biggest fundraising gala of the year. A temp cannot fill in for me right now."

"What do you expect to raise at the gala? A couple hundred thousand? I'll donate it."

"Money is not always the answer, Sander. I have a life I am building that means something to me."

"And I mean nothing to you?"

"What do you want to mean to me?"

He shook his head. "Is it so much to ask? I have offered two valid solutions and you refuse both," he said, refusing to answer the question that really mattered. Naturally.

"Neither of your solutions work for me. My role is to build connections with donors. Having someone fill in for me won't do that. You making a large donation won't do that either. What happens next year?"

"I am not going to commit to millions of dollars of funding for your org in order to convince you to come on a single trip with me."

"I'm not asking you to. That is my point."

"I cannot send someone else on this trip in my stead. Thousands of employees and investors rely on me to do my job."

"I know."

"So, why are you being so difficult?"

Rowan grabbed onto her patience with both hands. He wasn't being thick on purpose. It was just hard for the billionaire to understand that regular people had important commitments too.

Maybe she wasn't going to impact thousands of people by putting on a successful fundraising gala. That didn't mean it didn't matter though.

"I'm not trying to be difficult. I am your girlfriend, not your mistress. My life does not revolve around your schedule."

Lysander's expression went completely emotionless and a steel door slammed down between them with a clang that echoed in her heart. "I have never once said or implied that you are my mistress."

Oh, crap.

That was the wrong thing to say, but it was accurate, darn it. Lysander wanted her to drop everything, like a mistress who was expected to be on call twenty-four-seven, always willing to accommodate the important man's plans.

"I don't know why you are making such a big deal out of this, anyway. If this trip is anything like your work schedule since we returned to Greece, we'll barely see each other."

"You'll be there for me. Every night. In my bed."

Oh, heck no. "Are you sure mistress isn't the word you're looking for?"

"It is not just sex. Knowing I will be able to hold you through the night gives me comfort."

Something melted inside Rowan. That was no admission of love, but it was something much deeper than body driven lust. Maybe she could make the calls from Japan, although the time difference would make that problematic.

Lysander shook his head again. "Never mind. Clearly your job takes precedence. I will not ask you to compromise it again."

"Lysander."

But he'd turned away and was already making a call on his phone. That he was telling his personal assistant to take Rowan's name off the flight manifest, and cancel the employee fill in for her, made her heart twinge and her brain ignite with irritation in equal measure.

He had been so confident she would drop everything, he'd already made the arrangements for her to travel with him.

It was actually the pain in her heart that prevented her from chasing after him and apologizing. Or, worse, offering to figure out a solution that didn't leave her org hanging.

This arrangement of theirs was supposed to be no strings. More than sex. Less than love. No long term commitment.

Only her heart was already involved, bound to him with indelible bonds he had never asked for. And that scared her to death, considering how determined Lysander was to keep their relationship in the temporary category.

Rowan knew with everything in her that her feelings wouldn't end when their arrangement inevitably did.

Chapter Twenty-Six

Lysander joined Rowan for dinner but refused to be drawn into personal conversation.

Honestly, she didn't try very hard. Rowan was too busy attempting to come to terms with the reality that she was deeply in love with a man destined to let her go.

Seemingly unbothered by her own silence, Lysander reverted to his cold, ruthless business mogul persona. When the last dish had been cleared away, he excused himself to make some calls.

Eventually, Rowan went to bed. Alone.

How had they gone from the idyllic bubble they had ended the cruise in and brought back to Athens to this? Him so cold and aloof? Her so freaking doubtful and confused?

It took her a long time to fall asleep and when she did, it was fitful, not deep. She woke immediately when Lysander climbed into bed beside her.

He didn't reach for her like he usually did. Not to hold her. Not to initiate lovemaking. He didn't shift restlessly either. His breathing was even and deep. Was he already asleep?

Unwilling to let the distance between them remain, Rowan slid across the bed and put her hand on his chest. He said he found comfort by her presence in his bed. Maybe they both needed that comfort tonight.

Rowan softly kissed his shoulder and then sighed as she snuggled into his side. The unresolved conflict between them didn't stop her needing his closeness.

Lysander exploded up and came over her, kissing her with angry passion. Rowan's desire rose to match his and the kiss grew carnal as their hands roamed over each other's bodies.

"You are not my mistress," he growled as he surged into her body. "Even if you allowed me to support you in every way, you would be my girlfriend, not a woman kept in the sidelines of my life."

Oh, man. He expected her to talk now? To think?

Only, he clearly didn't, because when she tried to speak, he kissed her, pushing her words back with his thrusting tongue.

They were up for hours, sating their bodies with sensual pleasure in silence broken only by their erratic breathing and moans.

Every time she tried to talk, he stopped her. And part of her was grateful because Rowan was afraid she'd confess her love if she managed to say anything at all.

~ ~ ~

Lysander was gone when her alarm woke her the next morning. She didn't remember him kissing her goodbye, but that doesn't mean he hadn't.

Rowan had fallen into a deep, exhausted slumber after their last bout of lovemaking. She moved sluggishly as she got ready for work and would have been late if she had to make her own breakfast.

Thankfully, she didn't.

Helen had made her breakfast. It was waiting on a tray when Rowan came out of the bathroom, drying her hair with a towel. Vacillating between whether to text Lysander and tell him to have a safe trip, or not, she ate as she got dressed, and did her hair and makeup.

Finally, she decided to send the text.

Rowan: *Tell your pilot no risky flying. I'll miss you. Be safe.*

Lysander: *I will miss you too.*

Rowan didn't know what possessed her to send him three heart emojis. She wished she hadn't as soon as she'd pressed send. How obvious was she?

Her phone rang.

It was Lysander.

She answered. "Hello."

"I apologize for undervaluing your commitments."

Air whooshed out of her and it took her a moment to respond. "Thank you."

"You are important to me. Therefore, so are the things that are important to you."

"You're important to me too." Why were her eyes stinging?

"Sometimes we will have to be apart, but I will make a more concentrated effort to spend time together when we are both in Athens."

Rowan was too choked to say anything.

"Losing lucrative deals because of the time I spend with you is not going to sink my company."

Her laughter was watery. "Is that what happened?"

"My focus on business has not been what it was before we got together."

"I'm sorry."

"I am not."

"Oh. Well, then I'm glad." Did that mean he was coming to love her too?

Or was he resigned to being a less efficient corporate shark for the time they were together because he knew it wasn't going to last?

"I have to go."

"Okay."

"Do not forget to eat your breakfast. I reminded Helen to prepare you something."

"She did."

"Good."

"I..."

He waited in silence, but Rowan couldn't say anymore. She wanted to say those three little words that meant so much. Only she knew she couldn't. It wouldn't be fair to Lysander to burden him with her love when she'd agreed to a no strings affair.

That included bindings of the heart.

"I have to go too," she finally said. "Or I'll be late to work."

"Do not work too hard," he replied.

"You either." Though she doubted that admonition would be listened to.

They said goodbye and he disconnected the call, but he texted her later that afternoon to let her know when his plane was taking off.

Longing to be with him filled her. Had she been foolish to refuse to go with him? Their relationship had an end date. Why hadn't she jumped at the chance to spend every minute with him that she could?

Because for however long this thing between them lasted, she wanted it to be real. More than sex. More than his convenience. For however long they had together, they would be in a relationship.

A relationship in which they were equal partners.

It wasn't just about pride. It was about value. Her heart would shatter when they broke up, but she wasn't going to let him stomp all over it while they were still together.

Lysander would never play the role her family or her ex-husband had in her life. He would not dictate her schedule or her behavior.

Yes, she would compromise for him because he was worth it.

No, she wouldn't subsume herself to him, because *she* was worth it.

When her coworkers invited her for a drink after work again, she refused. As much as she did not look forward to going home knowing Lysander would not be there, she was not in the mood to socialize either.

She ate dinner by herself in the den, sitting on the sofa where Lysander usually sat and let the news play in the background as she read a book. Tired from the night before, she went to bed early, but found it impossible to go to sleep.

Until she pulled one of Lysander's dress shirts out of the laundry and put it on. Hugging his pillow and surrounded by his scent, she finally fell asleep.

Her phone woke her.

She fumbled for it and when she saw the unknown number, she considered not answering. What if it was Lysander? He should still be on his jet ten thousand feet in the air though.

Still, something told her to answer. So, she did.

"Hello."

"*Yineka mou*, did I wake you?"

"Sander. It is you. I thought it was, but I didn't recognize the number."

"Satellite phone on the jet."

"Oh."

"I wanted to wish you goodnight."

"Shouldn't you be sleeping? Tokyo is six hours ahead of Athens." She'd looked it up.

"Did you have a good day?" he asked, rather than answer.

Typical Lysander. He probably thought he didn't need sleep like other mere mortals. Arrogant, exasperating...*amazing* man.

"Yes. I found two big sponsors for the gala and talked to a couple interested in opening a branch of the organization in Thessaloniki."

"That is good news. What you do is important."

"Thank you for saying that." She put the phone on speaker so she could get more comfortable. "Tell me about what you're hoping to do in Japan."

"It is not a hope. It is a plan."

"Of course it is. And what is this plan?"

"I told Cyrus and my father that they would lose the deal they had going with the Japanese conglomerate. I worked on it while on the cruise, but I need to go to Tokyo to finalize the details."

"You're inserting your company in their place?" she asked. "Was that what you meant by losing money? Did you have to make concessions to push your father and Cyrus out of the deal?"

No wonder he'd been frustrated with her for refusing to go with him. Lysander was making this trip for her sake, to show his father and half-brother he'd meant business when he warned them off of her.

He was protecting her.

"No. My company brings more to any partnership than Andino Enterprises could. The conglomerate is happy to adhere to my requirement of cutting ties with my father's company in order to make a deal with me."

She didn't doubt it. She still felt guilty though. Because whether he was making money on this deal, or not, he was there for her.

"I wish you'd told me this was the deal you were using to show your father and Cyrus that they can't mess with me."

"I am glad I did not. You would have come with me out of guilt and there is nothing you have to feel guilty for. I take care of my woman."

Why did hearing him call her that in English send tingles through her body.

"You took very good care of me last night."

"As you did me." His voice had gone husky and deep.

She groaned. "I'm never getting back to sleep, am I? I should have just gone with you. I'll be a zombie by the time you get back."

"You will sleep tonight, I will make sure of it."

"How do you plan to do that?"

"Put your phone on speaker."

"It already is."

"Good. Now put both of your hands on those mounds I like to play with so much."

"What? We aren't doing phone sex, Sander."

"Cup them."

Why were her hands moving? As if he was moving them like puppet arms on a string, she undid the buttons on his shirt so it fell away to expose her breasts and the rest of her body.

"Are you doing what I said?" he asked.

"Yes."

"Rub your thumbs over your nipples. They're already hard like lush raspberries, aren't they?"

"Yesss." She drew the word out as pleasure washed over her. "Please tell me no one is there listening to you have sexy times over the sat phone with your girlfriend."

"No one gets to hear your sexy little sounds but me, *yineka mou*."

His voice went directly to her core, making it pulse, making her ache for him.

As if he could read her mind, he said, "Do not touch your vulva. Your hands stay where they are for now."

"Sander..." Was she begging? Or just saying his name?

She didn't know. Any more than she knew why she was doing what he said and why doing it was turning her on so much. She could feel the wetness gush between her legs, soaking her panties.

"Pinch your nipples."

She did and moaned at the sensations coursing through her.

"Harder."

"I can't." But she did and it sent a jolt of electric bliss straight to her center. Her vaginal walls contracted.

She needed him. But he was on a jet, hours and miles away.

"Slide your right hand down your body and into your panties. You wore panties to bed didn't you?"

"Yes."

"You don't when I'm there."

She didn't wear anything to bed when he was there beside her. Neither did he.

Her fingertip grazed over her clit and she gasped.

"Does it feel good, *glikia mou*? Do you know why I call you that?"

"Because I'm sweet?"

"Because you taste like honey."

"My mouth?"

"Mmm...and the nectar that flows out of your delicious little vagina."

She said a word she never ever said and he laughed.

Dipping into the wetness he was talking about, she drew it up to her clitoris, making it slick and easy to slide her fingers over. It felt, so, so good.

"Roll your nipple between your fingers while you touch your clit."

She did as he said, his voice sending sensations along her nerve endings just like her own fingers. Her orgasm took her by surprise, pulling a cry from her throat as her body bowed on the bed.

Even more surprising was the yawn that followed.

"Will you sleep now, *glikia mou?*"

"Yes," she said on a sigh, having an entirely different reaction to him calling her his sweet now.

It felt very personal. Very intimate.

"Good. I need to go take care of the hardon listening to you and imagining you in our bed gave me."

"Send me a picture," she joked and then yawned again.

She fell asleep almost immediately.

The next morning she found a text from him. No words. Just a picture of his still hard penis covered in his ejaculate.

Even as the image shocked her sensibilities, her mouth watered for his taste. She sent him her own text. A close up of her pursed, slightly parted lips with the words, *my mouth is watering.*

He texted back almost immediately. *I miss you.*

Not *I miss your mouth.* Not some kind of sexual inuendo. But *I miss you.*

This time when she sent him three heart emojis she didn't second guess herself.

CHAPTER TWENTY-SEVEN

Even though Lysander was in Tokyo and Rowan was in Athens, things were more like they'd been right after she moved into his villa.

They texted each other throughout the day. Even the six-hour time difference didn't stop him replying immediately to her messages, so she did her best not to send any after ten at night in Tokyo.

He video-called her every day at lunch to talk and every night at bedtime for other things. Which meant he was waking up at four a.m. to do it. Sometimes, he told her how to touch herself. Sometimes, she told him what she wanted to do to him, what she wanted him to do to her.

She always came and so did he. Rowan fell asleep afterward feeling wanted and cherished.

On Thursday, she went to her director and asked if she could work remotely the following week. Since she was working pretty much fulltime on the fundraiser, she didn't need to be in the office for her usual appointment sessions with the women her organization served.

The time difference wasn't insurmountable for her to make the phone calls she needed to, and any in-person meetings could be scheduled for the following week. She really could not have been gone the past few days, but she'd worked hard to make working remotely possible for the remainder of Lysander's time in Japan.

After some discussion and making sure her bases were covered, Rowan's director agreed. Then, she called Lysander's personal assistant and let the woman know of her plans to fly to Japan on Friday's redeye. Sounding relieved, the woman insisted on upgrading Rowan to first class and promised to arrange her return with Lysander on the company jet.

"I would have booked first-class if there had been any seats available, but there aren't," Rowan told her.

No, she wasn't a billionaire, or even a multi-millionaire like her ex-husband, but the divorce settlement was still sitting in her bank account, and she was prepared to use it to get herself to Lysander.

The PA harrumphed. "We'll see about that."

"Thank you for trying." She wasn't convinced anything could be done, but if anyone could get Rowan a first-class seat to Japan, it would be Lysander's terrifyingly efficient personal assistant.

"I'm very glad you will be joining him, Miz Johnson. He is so much happier when he gets to see you."

"Are you saying Lysander has been cranky this past week?" she asked, a little surprised. He was always warm and charming, not to mention dead sexy, on their phone calls.

"He is very much like his old self," the personal assistant said neutrally.

"Old as in before what?" Rowan pushed.

"Before you moved into the villa."

Rowan shouldn't be surprised her coming into his life had impacted Lysander. Moving in with him had changed her. A lot. She woke looking forward to every day. Even bad days were better because she got to see him.

Still, knowing he was different *did* surprise her. It also gave her hope.

She loved him. Could the change in him mean that he loved her too? Even if he did, would he ever allow himself to admit it?

Vulnerability was not her billionaire boyfriend's strong suit.

Rowan was making notes on a list of potential donors when her mother called and invited her to lunch. Her first instinct was to refuse. She didn't want to miss her video call with Lysander.

But then Vanessa Johnson pulled out the guilt card. "I have barely seen you this trip."

Before Rowan left Cyrus, when her parents had come to Athens, she had lunch with her mother a couple of times a week, at least. And since they had travelled in the same circles, Rowan had seen her parents at all of the social events.

Rowan had only been in Greece at the same time as her parents twice in the last year. The first time, she'd been learning to navigate her new life and thought she'd successfully found a compromise with them by attending a few social functions.

However, she and her mother had only had lunch together once the last visit and none at all this time.

"We're flying home soon. I wanted to see you before we do. Is lunch too much to ask?"

"No, of course not." She didn't particularly miss seeing either of them, but apparently her mother felt differently. "I'll warn you now that if you bring up Cyrus even once, I'm getting up and leaving."

"Really, Rowan, I didn't raise you to be so acrimonious."

"I mean it, Mom."

"Very well, no discussion of your husband. Can we make it an early lunch?"

"Yes." Rowan preferred it. She would text Lysander and ask him to video call her a little later than usual.

"Good." Her mother named a time and restaurant to meet.

"That's not your usual haunt," Rowan said with surprise.

The restaurant had an excellent chef but was small and out of the way. Not a spot to see and be seen.

"It's quiet and we'll get a chance to catch up without having to worry about paparazzi or running into acquaintances."

Particularly having an early lunch like her mother planned. Their social set didn't do lunch at eleven in the morning. That was for brunch and brunch wasn't done midweek at small eateries, no matter how good the chef.

Was it possible that her mother actually just wanted to catch up with Rowan? The idea made her smile. Although her mother's criticism had hurt over the years, she had also been the one parent who showed interest in Rowan's life both before and after her wedding to Cyrus.

~ ~ ~

Rowan was taken to the table where her mother waited as soon as she arrived at the restaurant. The dining room was practically empty.

Most Greek city dwellers ate lunch much later, but the restaurant served breakfast as well, so they probably saw little benefit in closing down when they might pick up some tourist business.

Not that it was anywhere near the typical tourist areas. Okay, she didn't know why they stayed open for what had to be a very quiet couple of hours midmorning. Did it really matter?

Rowan only knew she preferred the lack of people in case lunch didn't go well with her mother.

As soon as Rowan reached the table, Vanessa Johnson stood to hug her. It wasn't effusive and warm like Iona's hugs, but it wasn't entirely social fake either.

Vanessa sat down, carefully spreading her napkin over her lap. "I've already ordered our lunch."

"Okay."

"Do not look at me like that. I am your mother. I know the food you like to eat. I ordered you fish."

Rowan loved seafood and had to smile. "Thank you."

Although since coming to Greece, she'd learned that people typically ate their largest meal for lunch and lighter fare for dinner, Rowan wasn't surprised to see a small grilled fillet served with a leafy salad when their food was brought to the table.

Her mother had never approved of her curvier figure. Rowan was comfortable with her body though and that was all that mattered. Okay, it was pretty nice that Lysander found her sexually irresistible as well.

Without an iota of embarrassment, she requested pita bread to accompany her lunch and pointedly ignored her mother's look of disapproval.

Carbs were not her enemy.

Lunch was surprisingly pleasant without her mother making a single overt criticism. Discussion moved to her parents' upcoming social engagements and her mother asked if Rowan planned to attend any of the functions the following week.

"No." Rowan didn't explain that she would be out of the country.

That would only lead to more questions that would result in an argument if answered.

Any sense of pleasantness went right out the window when Rowan spied a familiar and unwelcome figure approaching their table. Adele Fournier.

Vanessa stood with a smile for the supermodel. Adele kissed the air beside both of Rowan's mother's cheeks in greeting before the women both sat down.

This had been a setup.

Unaccountably disappointed, Rowan tossed her napkin on the table and stood up.

Her mother grabbed her arm with surprising strength, halting her. "No. Do not leave. I invited Ms. Fournier to join us, and she took time out of her busy schedule to do so. The least you can do is listen to what she has to say."

"No." Rowan tried to pull her arm away.

"I really think you are going to want to hear what I have to say," Adele said, the French lilt to her voice no mask for the malice in her eyes. "More to the point, you will want to see what your mother has to show you."

"I doubt it."

"Rowan, please," her mother pleaded, appearing, and sounding genuinely distressed. "I'm only trying to look out for your best interests."

Whatever her mother's reasons for setting up this lunch, Rowan had no doubts that whatever drove Adele Fournier's presence, it was not altruism on the model's part.

The woman had stalked them to Mexico. Now she was going to...what? It was that *what* that had Rowan pausing. Forewarned was forearmed.

As much as she had no desire to spend a single minute in the other woman's company, Rowan cared too much about Lysander not to at least try to figure out what game the supermodel was playing.

While Rowan wouldn't believe Adele if she said the sky was blue, that didn't mean others wouldn't and Rowan wanted to protect her lover from being blindsided by the media if she could.

Her phone buzzed with a text. "Excuse me," she said to her mother and turned away before she swiped to see the message.

Sander: *I miss you.*

Love fluttered in her chest. They were going to video call in less than an hour, but he missed her because it was going to be thirty minutes later than usual. Or maybe he just missed her. Full. Stop. Like she missed him.

Smiling, she typed a reply telling him so before sending a second text to her bodyguard. She tapped on another app and then slid back into her seat before setting her phone on the table, face down.

Rowan looked at Adele with all the skepticism she felt. "You have something you want to say?"

"It's not going to be easy to hear." Rowan's mother patted her arm. She frowned. "Or to see."

Rowan wanted information, so she tamped down her immediate inclination to tell her mother she would never believe a word spoken against Lysander. Especially if it was said by Adele, a bunny boiler, if there ever was one.

"Adele is here as a favor to..." Her mother's voice trailed off. "To our family," she finally said. "But before she says anything, I need you to look at some photos."

Vanessa pulled out her phone. "These were taken this last week in Tokyo."

Tension stiffened Rowan's spine. This was going to be some kind of claim about Adele and Lysander in Tokyo. Someone had done their homework or had access to privileged information they shouldn't.

Yes, sometimes Lysander's trips were made public, but there had been nothing in the media, much less his company's social media alluding to his current visit to Japan.

Lysander wasn't just going to be annoyed; he was going to be raging.

"I admit I was surprised Lys asked me to join him on such short notice, but I had a break in my schedule." Adele's gallic shrug was perfectly executed to imply a lack of tension.

Maybe the woman should try acting as well as modeling.

Too bad she was playing to a wholly unreceptive audience. Even if Rowan and Lysander had still been arguing, she wouldn't have believed the narrative the supermodel was trying to create.

He had said no other women as long as they were together, and she had believed him.

She still did.

The calculating gleam in the model's eyes was subtle, but she was watching Rowan with unmistakable interest to see how she reacted to the story. Rowan *did not* roll her eyes, but it was hard.

"Let me see the pictures." She put her hand out for her mother's phone.

With a sad, almost pitying expression her mother handed over her smartphone. "Swipe right for additional photos."

The first one was a picture taken from a distance of Adele and Lysander looking very chummy while the model took a selfie with her phone.

"That's the café on the ground floor of the hotel we stayed in. The next picture is the hotel."

Rowan swiped right. Sure enough the next photo was a picture of the two of them in front of the hotel, again taken from a distance. There was a picture of them at dinner and one of the model coming out of a hotel suite Rowan assumed was the one Lysander was staying in.

There were even a couple of photos of them kissing, one through the sheers on his hotel suite windows taken with a telephoto lens. It was rather grainy and only someone who knew his build well would suspect the man in the picture was Lysander.

The other was in the back of a car, the driver standing beside the open door making the shot possible.

Each had a time and date stamp that coincided with the previous week. Rowan quickly sent all the photos to her own phone before handing her mother's back.

Chapter Twenty-Eight

"Where did those pictures come from?" Rowan asked, finding it difficult to keep her fury in check.

"Cyrus hired a private investigator to follow Lysander," her mother confided. "He didn't trust his brother not to be using you to get back at him."

Rowan almost laughed. If anything, it was the opposite way around.

Only, it wasn't. Not really. And never really had been. Whatever excuses Rowan had given herself for approaching Lysander, she was adult enough to acknowledge the real reason she'd shown up at his gate that day.

She'd wanted him and once her divorce was final, she could have him.

Rowan shook her head, hoping the older woman had been as taken in by the lies as Cyrus had hoped Rowan would be. Regardless of their strained relationship, she hated to think her mother was playing not only a willing but witting role in this farce.

Lysander didn't just get angry. He got even. And Rowan didn't like the chances of any of the players purposefully creating the false narrative coming out of this unscathed.

Rowan looked at Adele. "You want me to believe that you and Sander went from you being his platonic escort to necessary social events to having sex behind my back?"

She made no effort to disguise the skepticism in her tone now that she knew the details of the scam.

"Is that what he told you?" Adele trilled a mocking laugh. "That we only slept together once?"

"Adele, you said you wanted to help my daughter, not hurt her," Vanessa Johnson admonished.

The words surprised Rowan. It almost sounded like her mother cared.

"The truth sometimes hurts," Adele replied.

Rowan rolled her eyes. Cliché much?

"Surely by now, you realize what a powerful libido Lys has. Is it even remotely believable that he and I would have spent so many evenings together without having sex?" Her tone said: *Look at me, who wouldn't want to worship this?*

What Rowan realized was that Adele was a very proficient liar. Just like Cyrus.

Unfortunately for Adele and this little scheme she and Cyrus had come up with, Rowan was no longer the woman who had let herself be manipulated into a loveless marriage to a narcissist.

She'd grown in ways people like them would never understand. She knew her own value and *because* of her years with Cyrus and before that, growing up with her father, she knew the difference between a manipulative liar and an honorable man.

Lysander was the latter.

He'd told her that his relationship with Adele had been platonic after the one time of having sex. And him? She believed. 100%.

"I do know how deliciously strong Sander's sex drive is," she said now. "We've spent the last week having fantastic and very satisfying phone sex over video chat. You have not been in his bed."

Rowan's mother gasped. "Do not be vulgar. We are not here to discuss your...what you and Lysander do behind closed doors."

As amused as she was by her mother's clear embarrassment, Rowan was much angrier about the lies Adele was spouting and her mother's willingness to give them credence.

"But discussing his supposed sexual exploits with Adele is all right?" Rowan shook her head. "I don't think so."

Adele's face was pinched. The conversation was clearly not going the way she had expected.

"It is naïve to believe a man like Lysander Baros would be satisfied with that kind of thing. When he had a *companion* at hand." Her mother waived her hand, her discomfort with the topic clear.

Had she meant to make Adele sound like a sex worker? Considering the narrow-eyed look her mother cast the supermodel, Rowan thought the wording might have been deliberate.

The offended glare Adele shot Rowan's mother said she'd gotten the implication as well.

"Vulgar, or naïve, which is it mother? I'm pretty sure I can't be both."

"Do not let your heart rule your head," her mother said. "You cannot simply ignore the truth of Adele's claim and the proof of those pictures because you want to. You are smarter than that."

"I think you might actually be worried about me and not merely Dad's business relationship with the Andinos," Rowan said with surprise. "Regardless, you are right."

Her mother and Adele both perked up at that.

"I am intelligent. Intelligent to be aware of what a blatant liar Adele Fournier is. Smart enough to know that Cyrus has his own reasons for wanting to drive a wedge between me and Sander, but not one of them is for my benefit."

She stood up, done with this farce. "After living for most of my life with liars, I am savvy enough to recognize an honorable man. Sander promised me fidelity for as long as we are together and when he makes a promise, he keeps it."

Adele's tinkling laugh was mocking. "He's not a saint."

No. Lysander was no saint. He could be cranky and demanding. His pathological need to keep things tidy would be really annoying if he didn't have household staff. He was a workaholic and terrifically competitive. Possessive. Even jealous.

And she loved him with every fiber of her being.

"No, but he is a man who keeps his word."

"You're so sure?" Adele asked with more mockery.

There was nothing but certainty in Rowan's answer. "Yes."

Adele looked pityingly at Rowan. "You're a fool."

"Please, Rowan, I don't want to see you hurt," her mother pleaded.

Where was that concern when Rowan's father was feeding Cyrus information to make her fall for a man who had never existed? Where were those pleas when Cyrus cheated, and her parents were so adamantly opposed to Rowan filing for divorce?

Rowan shook her head. "I'm not the dangerously reckless one here, that would be you three."

Despite the immovability of her Botox treated face, her mother managed to look hurt. "For trying to protect you?"

"Let's leave the fact you're actually trying to make Sander's lover leave him and just address the reality that you two and Cyrus have conspired to slander a very wealthy, very powerful man who holds grudges."

"It's not slander! He is my lover," Adele claimed passionately.

"When was the last time you had sex with him?" Rowan asked. This was almost fun.

"Three nights ago, before I returned from Tokyo." Adele was cockily sure of herself.

"Let me be absolutely sure I have this right. Ms. Fournier. You are saying that you had sex with my lover, Lysander Baros, three nights ago in Tokyo?"

"Yes!"

Well, that was unequivocal. And Rowan was done. She picked up her phone, sent another text with attachments copied to Lysander and Klaus. Then she texted her bodyguard again, happy to see him materialize near the table within seconds of her sending it.

Her first text had been to tell him to come inside the restaurant and be close by in case she needed him.

Rowan stood and frowned down at her mother. "I don't know if you believe this charade, or if Cyrus has duped you into playing the part of concerned parent, but I hope for your sake it's the latter. It might save you from Sander's wrath."

"Those pictures! Rowan. You can't ignore them."

"Oh, I haven't. And neither will Sander." She glared at Adele. "I don't know if AI or CGI, or just plain photo manipulation was used, but Sander has the best tech experts on the planet working for him and they will find out."

Adele was trying to appear unaffected, but fear flickered in her gaze.

"I imagine you'll be hearing from his lawyers very soon, but I doubt that will be the extent of his wrath," Rowan drove the point home. "He once told me that when he knocks an enemy down, they stay that way."

"I'm not his enemy. I'm his lover!" the supermodel shrieked.

Unimpressed, Rowan continued, "You have stitched yourself up nicely and I think you know that Sander isn't a forgive and forget kind of guy."

After tapping her screen, the women's voices played from the phone's speakers, replaying the conversation they'd just had.

Adele leaped for the phone, screaming, claiming it was all a joke, but the bodyguard was there, and he didn't let the furious supermodel within a foot of Rowan.

"Rowan!" Her mother's distraught tone halted her. "You recorded us?"

"I did. I sent the recording and the photos to Sander already. Don't bother trying to convince me to keep this little drama between ourselves."

"I wasn't going to. But Adele and he...the pictures. After Cyrus...your own father. You know men cheat."

Hadn't she been listening? It was because of them that Rowan knew the difference. "Petty, insecure men with no honor cheat, Mom. Not men like Sander."

"You really believe in him."

"Yes." More than that, Rowan loved him.

However, the first person who was going to hear those words was going to be Lysander.

"I thought the pictures were real, that Ms. Fournier was doing us a favor by talking to you."

"Did you really? Or did you think that Cyrus had found a way to drive a wedge between me and Sander? I don't know why you think I would ever go back to that waste of space, but it will never happen. I don't care what that costs you and Father socially, or even financially. I'm done being a family pawn."

"Women do what they have to for their family, Rowan."

That sounded more like her mother.

Rowan just shook her head and walked away. She and Vanessa Johnson were never going to agree on what that meant.

One day, she hoped she'd have her own children and she would never, ever allow them to be used as bargaining chips.

She would never counsel her daughter, or her son for that matter, to stay with an unfaithful spouse.

Chapter Twenty-Nine

Lysander's phone buzzed with a text. Maybe Rowan had finished lunch with her mother early.

He grabbed his phone and opened their text thread.

Rowan: *Cyrus had (maybe still has) a private investigator following you in Tokyo.*

Several photos came through and each one increased the dread inside him until he was clammy with fear. An experience he'd never before encountered.

By the time an attached recording came through, he was throwing his clothes into the garment bag and barking orders over the phone to the top company executive he'd brought with him for this trip.

"You'll have to handle the rest of the negotiations. I won't be there."

"But Lysander, it's you they want to talk to. Mr. Takamasa made that clear. It's a respect thing. If you leave now, he could very well back out of the deal."

"I am aware."

"Good," the other man sounded relieved.

"Handle it. I'm flying back to Athens as soon as there's a takeoff slot for the jet."

The executive was still squawking when Lysander hung up and sent a barrage of texts to his people. He wanted the jet ready for takeoff within the hour and a takeoff slot arranged.

He told Klaus to get their techs on the photos to figure out what had been done to create them. He was sure his head of security was already looking into the PI working for Cyrus angle.

Then he dialed his brother's number.

"Lysander, to what do I owe the pleasure?" Cyrus asked, sounding so damn smug.

"I would have been happy to leave it at slapping your wrists with the land developer deal and cutting you out of the negotiations with Takamasa and his conglomerate, but now I will not rest until Andino Enterprises is in bankruptcy."

"What the hell? You can't threaten me, Lysander."

"It wasn't a threat." Lysander hung up and blocked Cyrus's number mid-ring.

His father's call came minutes later. Lysander blocked him too. If he lost Rowan over this, he was going to make sure that not only was Andino Enterprises destroyed, but he would burn his father and brother's entire lives down to ash.

Once he was on the way to the airport, he called Rowan.

~ ~ ~

Rowan's phone rang and she saw it was a video call from Lysander. Unfortunately, she was on another call, and she had to reject the video chat request. She'd been trying to connect to the woman well known for her philanthropic ventures the past two weeks.

She texted her lover to apologize. *Sorry I couldn't take your call. Talking to a potential donor. I'll let you know when I'm done.*

Twenty minutes later, she hung up from a successful call with the donor. The woman would be hosting a table at the gala as well as committing to a generous monthly contribution.

Wanting to share her good news and yes, curious to find out what Lysander thought of Cyrus and Adele's machinations, she tried to return his video call. It didn't connect and there was no text forthcoming.

He must be in a meeting.

A little deflated but reminding herself that she'd see him in person soon enough, Rowan went back to work.

Her phone rang again a half an hour later. It was the sat phone from the plane.

Rowan quickly swiped to accept the call. "Hello?"

"Rowan."

Sander. "Why are you calling me from the plane?"

"I'm flying home."

"Did you finish your negotiations then?"

"No."

"Then why are you flying back to Athens?" Seeing the time, she quickly closed down her computer and texted her bodyguard to bring the car.

"You ask me that after sending me those photos?" There was an odd quality to Lysander's voice.

He almost sounded a little unhinged.

"I know they're problematic, but do you really think they're that big of a deal? I'm pretty sure Klaus has it covered." That's why she'd copied him on the texts, so he could start working on the problem immediately. "Are you worried the Japanese conglomerate will back out because of them?"

"No," Lysander said, his voice strangled.

He was really upset.

"It's not like we're married or something," she soothed him. "Even if Adele or Cyrus sends them to the tabloids, the story doesn't have enough legs to make it onto the front pages, much less through a whole media cycle."

"I know we are not married, but I made you a promise."

"Just like I made a promise to you, but I don't think the media is going to care about that. Do you think Cyrus and Adele have been working together since Mexico? That's weird, right? Do you think they're together again?"

He cursed viciously. "I do not care."

"Are you okay? I know this sucks, but you sound more upset than I would have expected you to be." And he was flying home.

Like the drama his brother and ex-escort were trying to create was a lot bigger than Rowan thought it was.

"What is going on?" she asked as she stepped outside to find her bodyguard behind the wheel of the hybrid SUV Lysander had purchased for her use.

It was more comfortable for her bodyguard than her compact electric car, which was why she hadn't argued about using it. And it was a hybrid. So, there was that.

"Rowan..." he ground out. "Just be there when I arrive. Promise me."

Since he would arrive sometime in the early hours of the morning if he was leaving now, where else would she be? The trip from Tokyo was nearly fourteen hours and that was just the flight.

"I'm not waiting up for you," she warned him in a teasing tone as she buckled her seatbelt. "Though, I might as well admit I was going to fly out to Tokyo tonight."

If she didn't, he'd learn soon enough from his PA.

"You were coming here?"

"Yep. It took most of the week, but I got things settled so I can work remotely next week."

"You did not want to come with me."

"I never said that. I said I *couldn't* go with you. At least not this week." She sighed. "I know that concept is hard for your tycoon brain to take in, but some of us cannot make the world bend to our will on a daily basis. Honestly, Sander, I don't want to. Life might not always be convenient but fulfilling my obligations and making a way to join you was satisfying for me. Can you understand that?"

"Yes."

"You sound weird."

Looking out the window, Rowan was happy to note that her bodyguard had gotten the memo and they were headed to the villa and not the airport.

"Do I?"

"I guess we can talk more about our different approaches to life when you get back. Are you sure it's a good time to leave Japan? The deal won't sour, will it?"

"I don't give a..." He said a four-letter word that he almost never said around her. "I'm coming home. Those pictures are faked."

"I know."

"You know?" Lysander's voice was heavy with disbelief. "But you sent them to me."

"So you could be aware of the latest Cyrus gambit." Wait. "Did you listen to the recording?"

He didn't answer. Had the call dropped?

"Are you still there?"

"I'm here."

"Why haven't you listened to the recording?"

"When I got the pictures, I thought you were breaking up with me." The bleakness in his tone hurt her heart. "I thought the recording was a voice message telling me we are over."

"What the heck? Why would you think that?"

"You sent me pictures of myself with another woman. You said your ex-husband had me followed."

"Well, yes, I assumed you'd look into who the PI was. He had to be in your hotel to get the backgrounds he used for the pictures. I mean, I'm not excited about paying skeezballs, but you've got deeper pockets than Cyrus. The easiest way to prove the fakery of the photos and stop the story in its tracks is to get the PI to admit his part in it."

"Klaus is looking for the *skeezball* now. Is that another one of your Americanisms?"

"Most people say sleazeball but I like skeezball better. It implies sleazy and skeevy at the same time." She laughed, but it was forced.

He'd thought she was dumping him. And his response had been to fly back to Athens post haste. She hugged that knowledge to her heart. Maybe her three-word confession would not go unanswered.

Hope buoyed her heart. "You need to listen to the recording."

When he did, he'd have his own buoy because only a woman deeply in love would be so certain of her man's honor in the face of the evidence Rowan had been presented with at lunch.

"I will."

The silence between them was laden with words unsaid, emotions not given expression.

"Now," she prompted.

"Yes."

They hung up without saying goodbye. For Rowan there were only three words she wanted to say and she wasn't saying them until he was there, in the same room with her.

Chapter Thirty

R owan woke to soft kisses and whispered words as the sun was just beginning to rise.

Turning, she slid her arms around Lysander's neck and pressed into his hard, naked body. "Welcome home."

"Those words." He stilled, his eyes closed, his face a mask of emotion. "Say it again."

"Welcome home."

"This is our home. Yours and mine."

"Yes."

He opened his eyes, his dark gaze intently fixed on hers. "I listened to the recording."

"And?"

"You were never going to break up with me."

"No."

He swallowed, like he was trying to control strong emotion. "You *aren't* ever going to leave me."

"No. If you try to send me off, I warn you, it won't be easy. I've got squatters rights now to the den. Just ask my purse."

He frowned. "Did you leave it by the couch again?"

"Yep."

"You're a troublemaker."

"Not a slob?" she quizzed, arching against Lysander's body, inhaling his scent.

"I might be a little uptight about where things go."

"A little?" she teased.

"I admit that the purse wasn't the problem."

"Oh no?"

He kissed her softly and then shook his head. "No."

"Care to share?"

"You know."

"You didn't want to go to Japan without me."

"I didn't want to go to Japan without you," he agreed.

"Next time, lets focus on the real issue."

"I thought you didn't want to come, that you were getting tired of me."

"Funny, that's what I thought when you stopped working from home at all and I saw more of your staff than you."

He cupped her cheek. "I will never get tired of you."

"Promise?"

"Promise."

"That sounds suspiciously like a long-term commitment." She tried to tease, but her voice got all choked and Rowan had to blink back tears.

His answer was a prolonged, tender kiss, but when it started to turn hot and heavy, he pulled back and sat up against the headboard. "As much as I want you, we need to talk."

Rowan climbed into his lap, her knees on either side of his hips. "Maybe you shouldn't have come to bed naked then."

"I don't want any barriers between us."

That he was talking about things more important than clothing did not escape her.

"What do you want to talk about?" she asked.

There were more words she wanted to say, but for some reason they weren't popping out of her mouth like she'd expected them to.

"The recording."

"Adele overplayed her hand for sure," Rowan opined. "She was so sure I would believe her."

"I don't care about Adele."

"You don't?" Rowan asked. "What do you care about?"

"Ask me *who*."

"Who..." She had to clear her throat and take a deep breath before she got the words out. "Who do you care about?"

"You. *Agape mou*."

He'd never called her that before. It could be as innocuous as sweetheart, but in the right context, it meant, *my love*. Was this the right context?

"I care about you too." It wasn't all she wanted to say, but it was true.

"I know. You offer a loyalty that goes to the depths of your soul. You did not doubt me for even a second. You turned your recording app on immediately. You never once wavered."

"Of course not. You might be a workaholic and seriously grumpy about where I choose to leave my handbag for the next morning, but you would never lie to me."

Lysander sat up against the headboard, pulling her with him. "About the workaholic thing."

"Are you going to try to deny it?"

"No."

"I don't like the way things have been since we got back from Mexico." She wasn't dumping him because he worked long hours, but she wasn't pretending to be okay with it either.

"I didn't either."

She just looked at him.

"Yes, I know. It was my fault. I was trying to prove something to myself."

"What?"

"When you first moved in, it was easy to curtail my work schedule. I assumed our relationship would burn out quickly, especially if we lived together."

She'd half suspected as much, so she should not be surprised. Or hurt. She was both.

"I guess it worked." Rowan went to slide off his lap.

Lysander held her in place with firm hands on her thighs. "No, *agape mou*. Stay."

There was that endearment again. That little buoy in her heart bobbed, reminding her that he'd left an important business deal in Japan to come home when he thought he'd lost her.

"It did not work. In fact, the opposite happened. Having you here only made me crave you more. Not just in bed, though I will never get my fill of your sexy body."

The erection pressing up between them gave credence to this claim.

"Every minute we spend together is precious to me and only makes me want more minutes, hours, days, weeks..." He shook his head. "Just more. Since we returned from Mexico, I have tried to prove to myself nothing had changed for me."

Did that mean things *had* changed for him? She loved this man and if she wasn't deluding herself, he loved her too.

"Nothing about our relationship fit what I believed about myself. I have never been a jealous lover, but the idea of another man so much as looking at you makes me livid."

"You demanded monogamy though."

"Yes, and had no twinge of feeling if my sex partner decided to move on before I did."

"You wouldn't have let me go so easily." He *hadn't* let her go. He'd fought for the one night to become something more and for that more to become them living together.

"When the threats escalated and you were mentioned, I should have sent you away while I dealt with the problem—"

"Like that would have worked. I'm not going anywhere."

He grimaced. "I am aware of how stubborn you can be."

"Good. I wouldn't want you to be misled by my usually sweet nature."

He kissed her again, tasting her mouth for long minutes before pulling his head back. "You are sweet, *yineka mou*. Everywhere."

Her face heated with a blush, which felt silly because how many times had they made love? How many times had they explored each other's bodies thoroughly? She was sitting naked with him in bed and memories of why he called her *glikia mou* had her squirming.

His knowing expression said he was aware of exactly what she was thinking about.

But then he shook his head. "Later."

She sighed, but nodded.

"Instead of sending you away, or going to my New York office, I decided to use the need to get out of Athens to give you something you wanted."

"The cruise was amazing." Even with his hot-cold treatment and the stalker supermodel showing up as well as her ex-husband.

"I am glad you found it so. We can take another one in the future, if that is what you want." The words were so obviously forced, Rowan had to stifle an urge to smile.

"Once was enough. Thank you."

Relief washed over his handsome features. "If you are sure."

"I am."

"You need to understand that I've never put anything or anyone ahead of my business. Not even my mother. When I didn't even consider sending you away, much less going to my New York office, alarm bells went off. I ignored them. Just like I ignored my business to resolve the issue with those bastards as quickly as possible, so you were no longer at risk. The more I felt for you, the more I fought those feelings."

He'd been fighting himself, not her, which had led to his hot-cold treatment.

"That explains a lot. Is that why you threw yourself so intensely into work when we got back to Athens?"

"Yes."

"It hurt, but I understand."

"I never wanted to hurt you."

She believed him, but that didn't change the outcome. "I think when you love someone, they have the power to hurt you in ways you would never expect."

"Don't say it."

"What?" But she knew. Or thought she did.

"Let me say it first. I love you, Rowan. Your soul is entwined with mine and I will never let you go. I can't. To lose you would be to lose the other half of myself."

"That sounds like a lifetime commitment." Marriage.

"I'm not looking for a lifetime together."

"You're not?" she asked, her heart squeezing painfully.

"I want eternity."

Wow. Okay. Trust Mr. Billionaire Greek Tycoon to be an over achiever when it came to love too.

He reached for something on his bedside table and then put his hand out, offering it.

A ring with a huge yellow diamond surrounded by a cluster of marquis-cut smaller stones sat in the center of his big palm. "Will you marry me, Rowan?"

She couldn't get any words out; she was trying too hard not to cry. He hadn't bought that ring on the way home from the airport. This wasn't a spur of the moment thing.

"How long have you had that?" she asked, emotion clogging her voice.

"Since the day after you moved in."

She pushed herself up to look at him in shock. "You knew you wanted forever then?"

"I was still fighting it. I told myself it was a gift, not an engagement ring."

"But you never gave it to me." And that ring couldn't be mistaken for anything but the kind of bling a man gave a woman to claim her.

"Because no matter how I lied to myself, I knew giving it to you came with a question I wasn't ready to ask."

"I want children if we can have them." Images of a baby girl with his dark eyes, and a little boy with Lysander's chiseled chin filled her mind.

Rowan's ovaries clenched with anticipation.

"Is that a yes?"

"It's a negotiation."

He laughed, his eyes warm with the emotion she had no trouble naming now. Love. "I'm eager to hear your terms."

"My purse has a spot beside the sofa in the den."

"Done."

"I know you aren't going to work forty hours a week, but I need you to be present or there's no point in getting married." She wasn't having children to raise as a single parent either.

"I'm already working on a more manageable schedule. Losing a few million in deals is nothing in comparison to losing you."

From her tycoon? That was heart-meltingly sweet.

"I want vacations. A minimum of four a year."

"Done."

She gasped. She'd expected major pushback on that and had thought she'd have to settle for two at the most.

She narrowed her eyes. "A vacation is defined as seven or more days without working more than two hours a day."

He kissed her. "It will go in the prenup."

"Speaking of, there will be no monetary incentives, or otherwise for longevity or children in this prenup." That was becoming a common thing and she didn't like the cynicism of it. "Our staying together won't be because I'm looking for a bigger payout."

He didn't say *done* this time. He kissed her with voracious need. They made love and somewhere along the way, the ring ended up on her finger.

Afterward, while their hearts were still racing and her breathing was still ragged, she said the words, "Yes. I will marry you, Sander. I love you more than anyone or anything. I didn't know this kind of love was even possible. I've never felt it. Never seen it. But I feel it now. You are my everything."

"We are everything together."

"Yes."

"If you hadn't shown up at my gate, I would have gone looking for you."

That was a big admission for him, revealing a need and vulnerability that filled her with joy.

She owed him the same level of honesty. "I didn't come to you because I wanted revenge on my ex. That was my excuse, for myself and for you. I came because I wanted you."

She had always wanted him, even when she hadn't allowed her conscious brain to acknowledge it because she was married to another man. Lysander was it for her.

"I'm sure you realize by now that my suggestion we have an affair had nothing to do with Cyrus either." Lysander kissed her, his hand rubbing up and down the naked skin of her back. "I never realized what real desire was until I met you and you were married to my damned brother."

"Half-brother. You're not an Andino. You are a Baros and I love you, Lysander Baros."

Chapter Thirty-One

Rowan's mother called to apologize. Apparently, she had believed the photos were real and had been trying to protect her daughter for once.

If she could be believed.

"It was clear that you felt something much deeper for Lysander than you ever did for Cyrus. I wanted to save you the pain of years being married to a philanderer."

"You didn't feel that way about Cyrus."

"By the time you left Cyrus, he held no piece of your heart. He could not hurt you."

"Oh, it hurt all right." It had been the hurt of betrayal and not heartbreak, but it had been painful all the same.

"But you were not devastated. Not like..."

"Like what, Mom?"

"Like I was the first time I realized your father had a mistress. Our marriage was arranged by our parents, but he was so charming. So handsome. When he walked into a room, his presence filled it."

This was a side of her mother Rowan had never seen. "You fell in love."

"Yes, but he didn't."

"Why did you stay with him?"

"Because that is what women in our station did. Falling in love with Richard was my weakness to bear. My father had other women, but he and my mother were not unhappy. Later in life, they became devoted to each other."

"You thought that would happen with Dad?" Rowan had a hard time imagining her father devoted to anything but his own search for more wealth and power.

"Yes." Her mother sighed. "Your father wasn't like mine. He didn't mark our anniversaries or get me beautiful jewelry for my birthday."

Rowan remembered her father giving her mother money and telling her to buy something with it to show off at the country club more than once. She'd thought that was normal, so when Cyrus had done it for her first birthday as a married woman, Rowan hadn't been bothered.

Now, she was, but not on her own behalf. On behalf of her mother. Her mother was no saint, but Rowan's father was a real piece of work.

"The only time we socialized together was when he needed me by his side for his image's sake."

"I thought that was the way you wanted it." Her mother had never acted like it bothered her that she and her husband led such separate lives.

"After you were born, we stopped sharing a bedroom. I resented you for that, though it had nothing to do with you. You came six years after Michael. Neither of us was expecting me to get pregnant again. Your father was not pleased and refused to risk it happening again, so he moved me to another bedroom."

"That had to have hurt." Rowan couldn't imagine what it would feel like if Lysander tried to relegate her to a different bedroom.

She did know that she would make him regret it. In so many ways. Murder would not be out of the running for one of them.

Reining in her thoughts, Rowan asked, "Why not just use birth control?"

"I was on the pill when I became pregnant with you. I offered to get a tubal ligation, but he said not to bother."

Ouch.

Rowan saw so much about her mother she'd never seen before. The pain and discontent she'd been forced to live with day in and day out had manifested in the way she treated others. The resentment she felt toward Rowan for being the catalyst to losing what was left of intimacy in her marriage had made sure that Rowan got the brunt of that negativity.

It wasn't fair. And it wasn't okay. But she understood it now.

"We'll never be close, Rowan. I've made too many mistakes with you and we're very different people, but I never wanted to see you unhappy."

"I sure wasn't happy married to Cyrus."

"You seemed content."

"You really don't know me very well."

"No, I don't suppose I do, but that doesn't stop me being very glad you are happy now."

"Thank you." Rowan didn't know what else to say.

"Your father is very regretful that he backed the wrong horse in this race." Her mother's tone was almost gleeful.

"What do you mean?"

"He supported Cyrus's attempt to get you back, and even when he knew you were with Lysander, he assumed a man like him wasn't going to marry you."

"Now that we're engaged, he tried to leverage my relationship with Sander into a business opportunity, didn't he?" Lysander hadn't said anything, but Rowan could easily imagine how that meeting had gone.

"Yes. Your fiancée made it clear that he'd happily see your father begging on a street corner rather than ever go into a deal with him. Your father was livid."

"Sander is very protective of me."

"I am glad. You deserve that."

"This is weird," Rowan couldn't help saying.

Her mom's laugh was different than usual. It actually sounded like she was amused. "Yes. I imagine it is. It's taken me thirty years and being made a pawn by yet another scheming businessman to realize you were never the problem in my marriage."

"Uh...I'm glad."

"So am I."

Even after that phone call, Rowan was shocked when Lysander pointed out an article from a newspaper back home about her mother and father separating. Vanessa Johnson had moved out of the family mansion and filed for divorce.

She hadn't heard from either of her brothers in a couple of years, but the oldest sent a text demanding Rowan talk some sense into their mother. Her second brother sent her an email telling her that it was Rowan's fault their mother was doing something so bad for the family business.

If Rowan hadn't divorced Cyrus, apparently none of this would have happened.

Considering that both men had shown not a single iota of concern for their mother, Rowan ignored both the text and the email.

She kind of liked thinking her actions had spurred Vanessa's behavior. Rowan certainly wasn't ashamed of it. Maybe her mom would finally find some genuine happiness in her own life now.

~ ~ ~

Feeling bone deep contentment, Lysander cuddled his soon to be wife on the den sofa. Instead of a stock report, the television played a nature documentary about monkeys.

Rowan loved any kind of animal documentary and Lysander loved Rowan. Ergo, his unlooked for education about monkeys.

She shifted against him, unbuttoning his shirt so her hand could slide over his stomach. Usually, by halfway into whatever show they were watching, she had his shirt open and at least one hand on his bare skin.

It was a game he played with himself to see how long he could last before either pulling her to straddle him or throwing her over his shoulder and taking her to bed. Her complaint that she never got to see the end of her shows wasn't much of a complaint when accompanied by the heated look in her beautiful blue eyes.

"Have you figured out how Adele Fournier stalked us to Mexico?" Rowan asked, surprising him.

She hadn't seemed inclined to discuss the doctored images after the night they got engaged.

Lysander ran his fingertip over her ring. Soon it would be joined by a wedding band. That couldn't happen fast enough as far as he was concerned.

"She had a sexual relationship with one of my personal security detail and managed to put a tracker in his tactical watch."

Rowan sat up and climbed astride Lysander's thighs, her face filled with shock. "How did you find out?"

"Klaus discovered it after scanning every item the security team brought with them to Mexico. There is no way of knowing how long it had been in there, but they'd been having sex for months."

Rowan's brow furrowed and she shook her head. "Wow. That's some next level thirsty-stalking. The guy probably feels so used."

"What he feels is unemployed." And unemployable.

Klaus hadn't taken it well to find out one of his men had put Lysander at risk.

"You fired him? But Adele tricked him."

"Do not worry. She is getting her comeuppance as well." Fury surged through him when he thought of what the supermodel's machinations could have cost him. "She and Cyrus will regret trying to take you from me."

"You can be a little scary."

"Not to you."

"Never to me." Rowan's happy smile caused a much different feeling than anger to fill him.

"I'm thinking about selling my stock in Andino Enterprises to a competitor. I don't suppose you could help me with that?"

"It would be my pleasure."

"I can think of something a lot more pleasurable than facilitating a stock sale." She rocked her hips, rubbing herself over his rapidly growing erection.

They didn't make it to the bedroom.

Chapter Thirty-Two

Rowan was in her office at the org when she heard an unwelcome, but unfortunately too familiar voice in the hall.

Looking up, she found Cyrus standing in the doorway to the small room.

It was a Cyrus unlike she had ever seen before. He had several days stubble on his face. His hair was unkempt, his suit worse for wear.

"You have got to get him to stop, Rowan. He's going to bankrupt us."

Uh oh.

Lysander hadn't said anything about what he planned to do in response to Cyrus and Adele's scheme to convince Rowan he'd cheated. She'd only asked once, and he'd told her not to worry about it.

So, she hadn't.

But she'd never doubted for a minute that Lysander would accept the faked photos and spurious claims by the supermodel lying down.

"You knew your brother holds grudges, why would you risk his wrath trying to make me believe that garbage about him and Adele?"

"I didn't know he wanted to marry you!" Cyrus looked unhinged. "How would I? Lysander doesn't do commitment."

"Sucks to be you, I guess."

"Is that all you can say? We were married ten years!"

"But were we? Really? I mean if you negated our vows within hours of speaking them, how married were we?"

Cyrus shook his head like she made no sense. "Look, I don't care about the land developer deal."

He didn't care about losing out on the 3.5 million dollars Lysander had negotiated making the sale on her behalf?

"That's a lot of money, but then again, it's not." It had never made sense to her that Cyrus would go to so much trouble to try to get back together for a few million.

Her dad? He wasn't swimming in a pond as big as the one the Andinos were in. Richard Johnson would have fought harder for less, but not Cyrus.

"What do you care about?" Rowan asked.

What had driven Cyrus into showing up at her work?

"The stock shares. We need them, damn you, and Lysander is negotiating a deal for them with a rival."

"I know. I asked him to."

"You didn't even want them," Cyrus snarled. "You were going to waive all benefits from the prenup to get out of our marriage."

"I am aware." The judge had refused to allow it.

"So, sign them over to me now."

"No."

"What the hell do you mean? No?"

"I mean, you tried to take the man I love from me with a lie, just like all the lies you told while we were married."

If Cyrus had told the truth, Rowan would have divorced him long ago and would already be married to Lysander. They'd been connected from that first meeting and only her useless marriage had kept them apart.

"I need those stocks."

"Why?" she asked, only mildly curious.

"None of your business."

"Really? That's the way you want to play it when you're asking me for something?"

"We're trying to merge with another European company. I need those shares to meet the percentage vested requirement." Cyrus tried to look at her appealingly. "The merger is worth hundreds of millions to Andino Enterprises."

Like she cared. She'd been bartered for the good of that company and her father's, even though she thought she'd been getting married for the sake of love.

Rowan knew what love felt like now and was sad for her younger self that she'd been so easily fooled.

"That makes a lot more sense than you wanting to get back together when you never cared about our marriage to begin with."

"I need those shares, Rowan."

"It *really* sucks to be you."

"Get the hell out of my fiancée's office." Lysander was practically breathing fire.

Cyrus spun to face Lysander. "You're going to bankrupt us!" he accused. "Your own father's company."

"Did you think I would let you get away with trying to take Rowan away? You did not succeed and that is the only reason you're still breathing." Lysander's chilling tone probably terrified Cyrus.

It turned Rowan on to have all the fury focused on the idea of losing her though.

"Are you threatening to kill me?" Cyrus asked with disbelief.

"No. I am telling you what would have happened if the woman I love left me because of your lies."

"I just wanted the shares," Cyrus whined.

"Then you should have offered to buy them."

"I'll buy them now. I'll pay you twice what they are worth," he said to Rowan.

"Lysander has already found me a buyer."

"You heartless bitch!"

Lysander grabbed Cyrus, jerked him backward and then punched him so hard he made a dent in the wall when he hit it. "Apologize."

Cyrus told Lysander where to get off. It lost a lot of its impact because his tone was so nasally from his now broken nose.

Lysander yanked his half-brother up by his shirt and this time sent his fist straight into his solar plexus.

He dropped the now groaning and gasping man to the floor and put his hand out to Rowan. "We have an appointment with the lawyer to sign the prenup."

The prenuptial agreement wasn't anything like the one Rowan had signed with Cyrus.

There were no monetary incentives for longevity as she'd asked, but it spelled out quite clearly that what was Lysander's would now be hers. That if she filed for divorce, for any reason, she would get half of Lysander Baros's assets.

"I can't sign this."

"Why not, *agape mou*?"

"You're not giving me half of your wealth."

"No, I am not."

She breathed a sigh of relief, but then she frowned. "Was this some kind of test?"

"Not at all. Sign the document, Rowan."

"No. You just said—"

"You will never be divorcing me, nor will I ever end our marriage. The point is moot."

She wanted to believe that, but life had a way of taking unexpected turns. "It's not moot if it's in the contract."

"We can skip the prenup all together if you like."

"Not on your life." She wanted the promise of no more than 50-hour workweeks they'd agreed on, and four vacations per year, in writing. Signed by him.

"Then you agree to take half of my fortune if you ever leave me."

"I know what you are doing."

"What is that?"

"You know I'll never allow you to hand over half of your wealth and possessions."

"There is no handing over. What is mine is yours already. Nothing I have built would matter if you stopped loving me and walked away."

Tears burned her eyes. "Iona told me that under all that scary tycoon armor, beat a romantic's heart. I didn't believe her."

"It is not a matter of romance, but of truth."

"If you say so." She grabbed the contract and signed it. "You're stuck now, Sander. You're never getting rid of me."

The satisfaction that settled over his gorgeous features made her breathless. And wet.

His grin said he knew it too. "Are you ready to go home?"

"Yes."

~ ~ ~

They ripped off each other's clothes in the foyer and made love against the wall. She trusted him to have alerted the staff to give them privacy. He was efficient like that.

And it was a good thing, because once they started kissing and touching, Rowan's higher thinking skills went right out the window.

Afterward, he carried her to their bedroom. "I love you with everything in my ruthless tycoon heart, Rowan."

"Not nearly as much as I love you."

"Impossible." He made love to her again. This time in their bed with whisper soft touches, long slow thrusts and so many words.

Words about her beauty. About how much he needed her. About what he meant to her. About how perfect their children and life were going to be.

"Happy children aren't perfect," Rowan said.

"Then they will be imperfect, because with you as their mother, they can only be happy."

There were tears in her eyes when she told him she loved him again.

"Always and forever, Rowan."

"Always and forever."

Finis.

If you enjoyed Her Greek Billionaire, please consider leaving a review. Thank you!

Want to read bonus content, including a bonus scene for Her Greek Billionaire, and to be kept up to date on her books? Sign up for Lucy Monroe's .

Read more passionate contemporary romance by Lucy Monroe:

Read Lucy's new mafia romance series, .

With more than 10 million copies of my books in print worldwide (Isn't that wild?), I'm an award winning and USA Today bestselling author with over 90 published books. My stories have been translated for sale all over the world and after a long career in traditional publishing, I've gone indie. I am loving the freedom to write the stories both me and my readers enjoy the most. My new steamy mafia romance series, Syndicate Rules features the morally gray alpha heroes and spice I love to write. I write contemporary, historical and paranormal romance. Some of my books have action adventure and intrigue. All of them are spicy and deeply emotional. I'm a voracious reader and love to talk about both my books and those I've read (or should read...good recs are always welcome) on social media. Welcome to my world where love conquers all, but not easily!

For info on my books and series extras, visit my website:
www.lucymonroe.com

Follow me on Social Media:
Facebook: LucyMonroe.Romance
Instagram: lucymonroeromance
Pinterest: lucymonroebooks
goodreads: Lucy Monroe
YouTube: @LucyMonroeBooks
TikTok: lucymonroeauthor

ALSO BY LUCY MONROE

Syndicate Rules

CONVENIENT MAFIA WIFE
URGENT VOWS
DEMANDING MOB BOSS
RUTHLESS ENFORCER
BRUTAL CAPO
FORCED VOWS

Mercenaries & Spies

READY, WILLING & AND ABLE
SATISFACTION GUARANTEED
DEAL WITH THIS
THE SPY WHO WANTS ME
WATCH OVER ME
CLOSE QUARTERS
HEAT SEEKER

CHANGE THE GAME
WIN THE GAME

Passionate Billionaires & Royalty

THE MAHARAJAH'S BILLIONAIRE HEIR
BLACKMAILED BY THE BILLIONAIRE
HER OFF LIMITS PRINCE
CINDERELLA'S JILTED BILLIONAIRE
HER GREEK BILLIONAIRE
SCORSOLINI BABY SCANDAL
THE REAL DEAL
WILD HEAT (Connected to Hot Alaska Nights - Not a Billionaire)
HOT ALASKA NIGHTS

3 Brides for 3 Bad Boys Trilogy
RAND, COLTON & CARTER

Harlequin Presents

THE GREEK TYCOON'S ULTIMATUM
THE ITALIAN'S SUITABLE WIFE
THE BILLIONAIRE'S PREGNANT MISTRESS
THE SHEIKH'S BARTERED BRIDE
THE GREEK'S INNOCENT VIRGIN
BLACKMAILED INTO MARRIAGE
THE GREEK'S CHRISTMAS BABY
WEDDING VOW OF REVENGE
THE PRINCE'S VIRGIN WIFE
HIS ROYAL LOVE-CHILD
THE SCORSOLINI MARRIAGE BARGAIN
THE PLAYBOY'S SEDUCTION
PREGNANCY OF PASSION
THE SICILIAN'S MARRIAGE ARRANGEMENT
BOUGHT: THE GREEK'S BRIDE
TAKEN: THE SPANIARD'S VIRGIN
HOT DESERT NIGHTS
THE RANCHER'S RULES
FORBIDDEN: THE BILLIONAIRE'S
VIRGIN PRINCESS
HOUSEKEEPER TO THE MILLIONAIRE
HIRED: THE SHEIKH'S SECRETARY MISTRESS
VALENTINO'S LOVE-CHILD
THE LATIN LOVER 2-IN-1 with
THE GREEK TYCOON'S INHERITED BRIDE
THE SHY BRIDE
THE GREEK'S PREGNANT LOVER
FOR DUTY'S SAKE
HEART OF A DESERT WARRIOR
NOT JUST THE GREEK'S WIFE
ONE NIGHT HEIR
PRINCE OF SECRETS

MILLION DOLLAR CHRISTMAS PROPOSAL
SHEIKH'S SCANDAL
AN HEIRESS FOR HIS EMPIRE
A VIRGIN FOR HIS PRIZE
2017 CHRISTMAS CODA: The Greek Tycoons
KOSTA'S CONVENIENT BRIDE
THE SPANIARD'S PLEASURABLE VENGEANCE
AFTER THE BILLIONAIRE'S WEDDING VOWS
QUEEN BY ROYAL APPOINTMENT
HIS MAJESTY'S HIDDEN HEIR
THE COST OF THEIR ROYAL FLING

Anthologies & Novellas

SILVER BELLA
DELICIOUS: Moon Magnetism
by Lori Foster, et. al.
HE'S THE ONE: Seducing Tabby
by Linda Lael Miller, et. al.
THE POWER OF LOVE: No Angel
by Lori Foster, et. al.
BODYGUARDS IN BED:
Who's Been Sleeping in my Brother's Bed?
by Lucy Monroe et. al.

Historical Romance

ANNABELLE'S COURTSHIP
The Langley Family Trilogy
TOUCH ME, TEMPT ME & TAKE ME
MASQUERADE IN EGYPT

Paranormal Romance

Children of the Moon Novels
MOON AWAKENING
MOON CRAVING

MOON BURNING
DRAGON'S MOON
ENTHRALLED anthology: Ecstasy Under the Moon
WARRIOR'S MOON
VIKING'S MOON
DESERT MOON
HIGHLANDER'S MOON

Montana Wolves
COME MOONRISE
MONTANA MOON